OSLG

THE GHOST OF CHRISTMAS PAST

When a man is found dead in macabre circumstances, reverend's daughter Elizabeth Dearheart is thrown into a mystery. Who is the enigmatic Liam Doubleday, and what secret does he keep? Who is the mysterious Lucinda that seems to have haunted the dead man? As Christmas approaches, and Elizabeth begins to fall deeply in love, dark truths come to light and Liam's life hangs in the balance. Elizabeth must uncover the truth before losing him forever . . .

SALLY QUILFORD

THE GHOST OF CHRISTMAS PAST

Complete and Unabridged

LINFORD
Leicester

First published in Great Britain in 2013

First Linford Edition
published 2014

A catalogue record for this book is available
from the British Library.

ISBN 978–1–4448–2046–1

Published by
F. A. Thorpe (Publishing)
Anstey, Leicestershire

Set by Words & Graphics Ltd.
Anstey, Leicestershire
Printed and bound in Great Britain by
T. J. International Ltd., Padstow, Cornwall

This book is printed on acid-free paper

1

By the time Reverend Dearheart finished his sermon, the snow had covered the ground in a blanket of crystal white. The worshippers left the relative warmth of the church, and stepped out into a crisp winter landscape.

'How wonderful. A white Christmas,' said Mrs. Chatterbucks. She was a large buxom woman, accompanied by her sister, Miss Graves, who was as slender as her sister was round. 'I do so love a white Christmas, don't you, Miss Dearheart?'

Elizabeth Dearheart smiled. 'Yes I do. And so does Sam, don't you, dearest?' Elizabeth was a girl of quiet beauty, with almond-shaped brown eyes and fair curls, which despite her best efforts to keep them tidy, peeked out from under her bonnet. Her clothes, whilst not the height of fashion, accentuated her petite frame. She wore a thick blue coat over a modest pin-striped crinoline.

Her ten year old brother, Samuel, nodded eagerly. 'Can we make a snowman, Elizabeth?'

'I think we need a little more snow first.' Elizabeth turned her attention to the sisters. 'Mrs. Chatterbucks, Miss Graves. If you have no plans for the afternoon, you would be welcome to join us for luncheon. Father would be so grateful for the extra company. He always says the vicarage is far too quiet.'

The invitation was always couched in such terms, so that the impoverished sisters were not offended by the hint of charity. 'I daresay we can save our food for another day,' said Mrs. Chatterbucks. 'What says you, Henrietta?'

Henrietta Graves nodded her assent. 'Yes, Georgiana dear, I'm sure we may.'

'It just so happens,' said Mrs. Chatterbucks, 'that I forgot to put the roast in the oven before we left. One gets so absent-minded at my age.'

Elizabeth guessed there was no roast, and that the sisters would have probably dined on bread and cheese, but she said nothing.

'Ah, here are Doctor Wheston and his wife,' said Mrs. Chatterbucks. 'Good morning, Doctor.'

'Good morning, Mrs. Chatterbucks. Miss Graves.' He raised his hat, and his wife, a pretty young woman some years younger than he, smiled and nodded her head. 'Tell your father we very much enjoyed his sermon, Miss Dear-heart.'

'Thank you,' said Elizabeth. 'He'll be pleased to hear it. I hope you're both settling in.'

'Yes, thank you,' said Mrs. Wheston. 'Midchester is a charming village.'

'We think so,' said Elizabeth. 'Perhaps you could come to dinner one night. And of course,' she added, seeing Mrs. Chatterbucks's keen expression, 'you and Miss Graves would be most welcome too.'

'Well yes, we would,' said Mrs.

Chatterbucks. 'The thing is, Doctor Wheston, we've been reading all about the Demon Doctor of Delhi. And I said to Henrietta that if anyone would know how he managed to dispose of the body, then Doctor Wheston would. There are probably ways, known only to doctors.'

Elizabeth looked at her brother, Samuel, who was listening avidly. 'I don't think . . . ' she started to say.

'And now,' interrupted Miss Graves with grim relish, 'they say he has escaped. We could all be murdered in our beds.'

'That is hardly likely, considering he is in India, and we are in a small town in Shropshire,' said Doctor Wheston. His lips had set in a thin line, and Elizabeth noticed that his wife clung to his arm so hard that her knuckles had turned white.

'Are you well, Mrs. Wheston?' she asked, hoping to change the subject.

'No, I'm afraid I am not,' said Mrs. Wheston. 'Such talk distresses me.'

'Oh do forgive us, Mrs. Wheston,' said Mrs. Chatterbucks. 'My sister and I take great pleasure in reading about famous murder cases.'

'I hardly consider murder a pleasurable pursuit,' said Doctor Wheston. 'If you'll excuse me, I must take my wife home.'

Elizabeth watched with concerned eyes as they left the churchyard. 'Well really,' said Mrs. Chatterbucks. 'I would not have expected a man of medicine to be so sensitive.'

'Dearest,' said Miss Graves, her eyes gleaming. 'You don't suppose that Doctor Wheston is he, do you? I mean, he is new to Midchester and . . . '

'Considering that the Demon Doctor of Delhi's wife is supposed to have taken her own life after his incarceration, it is unlikely,' said Elizabeth. She spoke lightly, so as not to sound too judgemental. 'Mrs. Wheston looks very much alive to me.' It wasn't that Elizabeth was against a bit of gossip. Mrs. Chatterbucks was right in that living in such a quiet town, one looked to the outer world for excitement, but even she understood how serious it would be if they began a whispering campaign against Doctor Wheston. Gossip spread through a small town like an untended fire, destroying innocent people in its wake. 'Besides, Father has known him for many years, and it was he who suggested Doctor Wheston take up the post here.'

'Oh yes,' said Miss Graves. 'I had forgotten that. But still, it's strange that he should be married to such a young woman.'

'He's a fine-looking man,' said Elizabeth. 'Why should he not have a younger wife? My dear mother was fifteen years younger than my father.'

'Of course,' said Mrs. Chatterbucks, 'Henrietta has never married, nor been in love, so she little understands how attractive an older man can be, Miss Dearheart. Take my Herbert. He was twenty years older than I, but a more appealing man you never did see.'

Having seen the late Herbert Chatterbucks, Elizabeth could not see the appeal herself, but she had heard that love was blind.

'And now here's another fine-looking man,' said Mrs. Chatterbucks as Mr. Charles Hardacre left the church, deep in conversation with the Reverend Dearheart. 'Good morning, Mr. Hardacre. I see Miss Dora is not with you this morning.'

Mr. Hardacre raised his hat, and saved his most charming smile for Elizabeth. He was tall, and considered very handsome by the women of Midchester for whom there were few choices of eligible men. 'Sadly no, Mrs. Chatterbucks. My sister is unwell today, and has taken to her bed.'

'Oh the best place for her,' said Miss Graves. 'One cannot risk catching a chill in this weather. Why only the other week the butcher's wife died from a fever.'

'Yes, and the week before that, I heard that a woman over in Clun died of pneumonia,' said Mrs. Chatterbucks.

'Yes, well, I'm sure Miss Clara isn't that bad,' said Elizabeth, quickly. She looked at Mr. Hardacre with an apology in her eyes. 'At least I hope not.'

'No, most certainly not. But as you so rightly say, Miss Graves,' he said, 'one must be careful.'

'I've just asked Mr. Hardacre to join us for luncheon,' said Reverend Dearheart.

'Oh yes, how wonderful that would be. I'm sure Miss Dearheart thinks so,' said Mrs. Chatterbucks. She and her sister exchanged conspiratorial smiles.

'Alas, I must refuse your charming company and return home to my sister,' said Mr. Hardacre.

'What a wonderful, attentive brother he is,' said Mrs. Chatterbucks, as they all walked to the vicarage. 'And a good catch for the right young lady.' She glanced across to Elizabeth.

'Yes indeed,' said Miss Graves. 'After all, one cannot leave these things too long, for life is very short.' She also gave

Elizabeth a meaningful look. Elizabeth ignored them both. 'One never knows when the Good Lord will take us.'

'I hope He will at least allow us time to enjoy our luncheon,' said Reverend Dearheart as they reached the vicarage door. 'Now, tell me ladies, what new murders have you been reading about lately?'

'Father, I don't think Samuel needs to know, do you?' Elizabeth muttered, whilst the sisters were busy divesting themselves of their outdoor clothing.

'Oh I don't mind,' said Samuel. 'I find murder most interesting.'

'That's because you only know about it from afar, dearest,' said Elizabeth, taking off her own bonnet. 'It would be quite different if someone close to you were murdered.'

'I don't think anything like that will ever happen in Midchester,' said Miss Graves. She sounded more disappointed than seemed proper.

Elizabeth showed the ladies into the pretty parlour, where they immediately stood by the roaring fire, warming their cold hands. She thought of the tiny cottage they lived in, full of drafts and with a leaky roof, and tried to feel kinder towards them. Their life was a hard one.

During luncheon, they regaled Samuel and the reverend with more tales of murder and early death, though the Demon Doctor of Delhi was clearly their biggest interest.

'They say he embezzled a patient's money,' said Mrs. Chatterbucks. 'An Anglo-Indian major who was a man of good standing and great honesty. Sadly, he had become senile. Then when the doctor feared his crimes would be discovered, he . . . '

'Oh do let me tell this part, dear,' said Miss Graves, her eyes glowing with relish. 'He murdered the major with an overdose of sleeping draught.'

After luncheon, the ladies dozed a little over coffee in the parlour, whilst Elizabeth and her father helped their maid, Abigail, with the clearing up.

'Really, Miss Dearheart, Reverend, it isn't right you should have to do this,' said Abigail. 'I'm the servant. Really, sir, a gentleman should not have to dry his own dishes'

'You're a servant who's severely overworked,' said the reverend. 'We don't know where we'd be without you, Abigail.'

'I don't say that isn't true,' said Abigail, smiling. 'But you really should sit and rest. Both of you. Leave this to me.' Neither Elizabeth nor the reverend listened to Abigail. They knew she liked the company, and to hear the latest gossip.

'I do wish the sisters were not so bloodthirsty,' Elizabeth said to the reverend, handing him a plate to dry. 'It isn't good for Samuel to hear it all. And you should not encourage them.' She smiled. It was hard for her to be angry with her father.

'Samuel is a very sensible young man,' said the reverend. 'As for the sisters, I believe their relish is more to do with relief than pleasure in other's misfortune.'

'Relief?' Elizabeth frowned and raised an eyebrow.

'Yes, they're old and poor, and wear threadbare clothes, but every year they survive whilst others around them die. Their prolonged life is their only wealth. All they can do is relish their own survival. Besides, my dear, I've seen you reading Wilkie Collins's stories. What's the latest one? 'The Woman in White'?'

Elizabeth grinned. 'Yes, all right, I admit to enjoying a good mystery, but at least that isn't real.'

'But the murders which the sisters read about aren't real either. Yes, I know, they are.' He held up his hand to halt Elizabeth's protestation. 'I understand that someone really dies, but the fact that it's there, in black ink on white paper, much as novels are, makes it seem unreal to them. Just words on a page.'

'So you don't think it's wrong of them?'

'How could I? After all, what is the Bible if not a collection of stories about murder and betrayal?' The reverend raised a finely arched eyebrow.

'*Touché*,' said Elizabeth.

When the sisters had woken from their nap, Elizabeth and Samuel offered to escort them back to their cottage. 'Abigail appears to have made too many pork pies for Christmas,' said Elizabeth, as they were putting on their coats. 'We shall never eat them all. Would you be kind enough to take a couple off our hands?'

The sisters accepted magnanimously, and left the vicarage clutching one pork pie each.

★　★　★

The snow had been falling fast, and they walked out into a winter wonderland. It made the world seem silent. Somewhere in the distance they heard a shotgun blast, then a piercing cry. 'What was that?' said Samuel.

'It was probably a bird,' said Elizabeth, yet despite her assurance to Samuel, the otherworldly cry made her shiver. She put it down to the snow, and the changes it made in the atmosphere.

'Elizabeth?'

'Yes, Sam?'

'When we've shown Mrs. Chatterbucks and Miss Graves to their door, can we go and see if the pond is frozen? Then tomorrow me and Johnny Fletcher can go skating.'

With a promise that they could, Samuel skipped on ahead, picking up snowballs as he went and throwing them without aim at various walls and trees, whilst Elizabeth and the sisters followed at a more sedate pace.

'Do you think it was a bird?' asked Miss Graves, for once waiting until Samuel was out of earshot. 'It sounded very much like a man screaming. Perhaps he was being murdered.'

Elizabeth sighed. 'I'm sure Midchester is the last place in which to find a murderer, Miss Graves. Nothing exciting ever

14

happens here.' It was only as she said it that Elizabeth realised that she wished something exciting *would* happen. She was happy enough in her life, but . . . well, she had to admit that sometimes she wished for more than the daily chores at the vicarage and the inevitable Sunday afternoons in the company of the sisters. She thought of Charles Hardacre and his sister, Dora. They at least brought some glamour to Midchester. It was said they were the nephew and niece of a famous duke, though they were far too discreet and principled to drop his name into conversations.

'Here we are,' she said, with more relief than she intended. They had reached the door of the sisters' cottage. 'Thank you for joining us today. Perhaps if you are not too busy next Sunday, you could join us again.'

'We will have to see, Elizabeth,' said Mrs. Chatterbucks. 'One gets so many invitations . . . ' She left the rest unsaid, perhaps because it might have turned into an even bigger lie. 'But of course, you and the dear reverend will always come first with us.'

'Come along, Samuel,' said Elizabeth, after she had said goodbye to the sisters. 'It will be dark soon, and we don't want to be out too late.'

'Can we go home past the pond, Elizabeth?'

She was hoping he would forget. Despite her earlier wish for excitement, she suddenly felt the urge to sit in front of the fire with a good book and a warm blanket over her knees. Something made her feel uneasy. She could only link it back to the dreadful scream they had heard. She pushed the thought away. They lived in the countryside, where there were always sounds of animals and birds, not to mention the occasional shotgun blast from poachers and gamekeepers. Why today's noise should make her feel any different, she did not know.

'Very well, but quickly, darling. It's terribly cold out and you don't want to catch a chill.'

'No,' said Samuel, affecting Miss Grave's voice, 'for then I might get ill and go to my grave early. For one never knows when He will call you.'

Elizabeth wanted to laugh, but a sudden and terrible sense of foreboding stopped her. 'Please don't joke about such things, Sam.'

It was only as they got nearer the pond, which was on the outskirts of the town, just below a wooded copse, that she realised why she felt afraid. That was the direction from which the scream had come. The sky was beginning to darken, and the snow still fell. Her instinct was to turn back, but they had reached a point where it was quicker to go home past the pond than it was to turn back and take the other route.

'Oh look,' said Samuel. 'I think someone has built a snowman. I bet Johnny Fletcher has already been out. Oh it is too bad. He might have asked me to join in.'

Sure enough, ahead of them was a man made of snow, standing some three feet off the ground. 'It certainly looks like he beat you to it, dearest,' said Elizabeth. But all the same, something about the snowman unnerved her. He appeared to be in a kneeling position, with his legs beneath him. She had never seen a snowman built in such a way.

'Wait there a moment,' she said to Samuel, putting her arm on his shoulder. 'Don't go any nearer.' She moved towards the snowman and crouched down next to him. A thick dark patch had seeped through the snow near to the snowman's chest. Tentatively, she put her gloved hand on the snowman's leg, and pressed down. As she did so she heard him groan.

'Samuel,' she said, as calmly as she could, though her heart hammered in her chest and she could see her quickened breath escaping from her mouth in clouds of steam. 'I want you to run and get Father. No, go to Doctor Wheston, then to Father. Oh hurry, dearest.'

Samuel stared for a moment, and

then ran as if he had the hounds of hell chasing him.

She brushed the snow from the man's head, and he opened his eyes briefly. 'Lucinda,' he whispered.

'Please, try not to speak; the doctor will be here soon.' She took off her coat and put it on the ground behind him, before helping him to lie down.

On hearing footsteps in the snow, she looked up and saw a man approaching them. He was dressed in a thick dark coat and wore a wide-brimmed hat, so that in the dim light she could not see his face properly. All she could make out was that he was very tall, well over six feet, and had broad shoulders. There was something about him that unnerved her, yet she had to admit that it was not an unpleasant feeling.

'What is it?' the man asked. 'What has happened?'

'This man has been hurt,' said Elizabeth. 'I think . . . I think he has been shot. Then someone covered him with snow. I can hardly believe anyone would do such a dreadful thing.'

'Let me look at him.' His deep voice held the hint of an Irish accent. It was most attractive.

'My brother is fetching Doctor Wheston. He should be here soon.'

'I am a doctor,' he said in calm, professional tones. 'Let me see.' The stranger crouched down on the other side of the stricken man. 'Do you know this man?' She could see the doctor's face more clearly. She guessed that he was in his early thirties, and unlike many of the men she knew, was clean-shaven, with short, dark hair.

'No, I have never seen him before.' For the first time, Elizabeth looked at the injured man properly. He was a man of middle age, portly, and with a fine set of whiskers. 'But he just said a name. Lucinda.'

The stranger glanced up at her, whilst tending to the stricken man. 'Do you know a Lucinda?'

'No, there is no one in Midchester of that name. At least not that I know of.'

'I daresay that Midchester is the sort of town where everybody knows everybody else.' He spoke wryly.

'Yes, it is rather. It's strange but I was only wishing today for some excitement. Now . . . '

'You would do better to wish for peaceful evenings and quiet nights, Miss . . . '

'Dearheart.'

'Dearheart?' He smiled, and she felt her heart flip. 'That's a very appropriate name for you. This poor man has been shot. I'm afraid the wound might be too near to the heart.'

'Elizabeth!' She heard her brother's voice behind her. 'I've brought Doctor Wheston.'

Doctor Wheston approached them then stopped suddenly. It was not at the injured man he looked, but at the stranger.

'Hello, John,' said the stranger, standing up. 'I warrant you did not expect to see your old friend Liam Doubleday here.'

'Liam? Of course.' He held out his hand, and took Liam's. Their greeting was full of intensity and unspoken words, making Elizabeth feel that she had arrived in the middle of a conversation. 'You should have told us you were coming. Amelia will be . . . surprised. And absolutely delighted. What do we have here?'

Whatever surprise Wheston might have felt on seeing his friend, his professionalism took over.

'He's been shot in the chest,' said Liam. 'I've done what I can to stem the flow of blood, and thankfully the snow has helped, though whether his assailant thought of that is another matter. But we need to get him out of the cold so we can treat him properly. This young lady . . . ' he looked at Elizabeth, 'says that he mentioned the name Lucinda. Do you know of a Lucinda in this area?'

Wheston appeared to think about it very carefully. When Wheston replied, he spoke guardedly. 'No, there are no

Lucindas here that I know of.'

At this the man on the ground grasped Elizabeth's hand and pulled her down to him. 'If not Lucinda, then her ghost,' he said. His eyes closed, and he was dead.

2

Over the next few days, the news of the stranger's death spread through Midchester faster than the snow, seeping under every door alongside the sharp winter winds. Some said he was a spice trader from the West Indies, involved in shady deals. Others said he was a government inspector who had been murdered to stop him from reporting farmers who were less than honest about their taxes.

'It's so exciting,' said Mrs. Chatterbucks. Elizabeth had met the sisters on the way to her aunt's. Despite the extreme cold, they loitered in the town square, desperate to discuss the murder with anyone, having gone over it between themselves so many times already. 'A real-life murder in Midchester.'

'It's actually very sad,' said Elizabeth. 'It was a horrid way to die.'

'Was it, dear?' asked Miss Graves, her eyes hungry for details. 'Of course we don't know all the particulars, but is it true that he had been formed into a snowman, complete with a carrot for a nose?'

'No, that is not true,' said Elizabeth. She spoke politely but firmly. 'At least not the part about the carrot. I really don't think I should talk about it. I told Constable Hounds everything.'

'Oh, well I suppose that's for the best,' said Mrs. Chatterbucks, sighing with disappointment.

'Do you have any idea who he might have been?' asked Elizabeth.

'Why no, dear,' said Mrs. Chatterbucks. 'As if we would have anything to do with a murdered man. The very thought is scandalous. If Mr. Chatterbucks were still alive, he would say the same thing. Once, when we were first married, a man we called a friend was murdered by a vagabond. To think we invited him into our house, and that he ate at our table.' Despite her pretended horror, Mrs.

Chatterbucks seemed to be relishing her connection with the dead man.

'I hardly think it was the poor man's fault he was murdered,' Elizabeth said sternly.

'Oh, I don't know about that,' said Miss Graves gleefully. 'Some people do rather bring death upon themselves.'

'I should really be getting on,' said Elizabeth with a sigh. Why the sisters should annoy her more than usual she did not know. It did not help that her thoughts kept going back to Doctor Doubleday. Her normal restlessness, which she managed to keep under control most of the time, had increased tenfold since she met him. 'My aunt is expecting me.'

'Do give our best regards to Lady Bedlington,' said Mrs. Chatterbucks. 'Of course, we have never dined with her, but I hear she keeps a very good table.'

The hint was a familiar one to Elizabeth. Bidding farewell to the sisters, she continued on to Bedlington Hall.

★ ★ ★

'Is that you, Elizabeth?' Her aunt lay in the centre of a large bed, in a darkened boudoir, surrounded by various bottles, from which she partook regularly. She said they were medicine, and that might have been true of some of them. Others smelled distinctly alcoholic, and her aunt had a tendency to call them embrocations. Elizabeth doubted they had ever been used as liniments.

Lady Bedlington's true age was a secret known only to herself. She looked ninety, but as it was often said she had been born middle-aged, she might only be fifty. She was Elizabeth's great aunt, the sister of her father's mother.

'It is, Aunt Arabella.'

'You are late. I will not stand for lateness.'

'I was talking to Mrs. Chatterbucks and Miss Graves.' Elizabeth unpacked the basket of food she had brought for her aunt. She did not apologise, believing that it only made her aunt feel more powerful.

'Oh don't mention those silly women to me. A couple of prattling idiots, both of them. I daresay they've tried to get an invitation to Bedlington Hall again.'

'Yes, actually, they did. It would mean an awful lot to them, Aunt Arabella.'

'My nerves could not bear it. I have not your patience, Elizabeth. Now tell me, is it true what I hear? That there has been a murder?'

Given her aunt's hermit-like existence, it surprised Elizabeth that she knew anything at all. She told her aunt the details, including a description of the dead man.

'That sounds like George Sanderson. Goodness knows what he's doing, getting himself murdered. As if his family hasn't enough problems.'

It occurred to Elizabeth that the sisters and her aunt should get on rather well, given that they all had a tendency to blame misfortune on the victims. 'You know him? Perhaps you should tell Constable Hounds.'

'I most certainly will not. There will be no policeman in this house.'

'Surely you want to see justice done.'

'It has managed quite well without my interference for many years.'

Elizabeth would have liked to disagree. All around her she saw injustices taking place, particularly to those who could not afford to pay for proper counsel.

'Perhaps you could tell me about Mr. Sanderson,' said Elizabeth. Her idea was that she could go to Constable Hounds and tell him to check if Mr. Sanderson was the dead man.

She sat on the edge of the bed, having finished unpacking the delicacies. She could have left them in the kitchen with the servants, but as her aunt didn't trust servants not to eat the best food, she insisted on seeing anything brought to the house first. Elizabeth knew that when she left, Lady Bedlington would take out a little notebook and make a list of it all. Then she would tick everything off as it was served to her. It seemed to Elizabeth to be a sad way to live, always worried that someone would steal from you. And given that Lady Bedlington could afford enough food to feed the whole town for a year, it also seemed somewhat miserly. Why should the servants not share in some of the pork pie? Lady Bedlington had the appetite of a sparrow.

'Why should you want to know? That is your trouble, Elizabeth. Too inquisitive. Of course, if your mother had been high-born, you would know that it does not do to show one's ignorance by asking too many questions. I did warn Philip. A reverend needs a wife who can be a credit to him.'

Elizabeth struggled to control the anger that rose within her. Her late mother, though from the lower classes, had been gentle, kind and intelligent, and beloved by her father's parishioners. She had died giving birth to

Samuel, having lost many children in between, leaving Elizabeth, at the age of fourteen, as foster mother to a baby boy. 'My mother was a credit to Father and to Midchester,' said Elizabeth firmly. 'Now, please, Aunt Arabella. Tell me about Mr. Sanderson.' She was surprised by the command in her own voice. Especially when it appeared to have the desired effect.

'He is, or was, an architect from Devon, and has often worked on our properties down there. A troublesome family, the Sandersons, but I daresay he does his work well enough. I called him up to discuss building an orangery onto Bedlington Hall. Now he is dead, I suppose I shall have to start all over again. It is most inconvenient.'

'You said his family was troublesome. In what way?'

'Insanity. It's rife in that family. Mr. Sanderson's mother became an imbecile soon after giving birth to Mr. Sanderson's brother, Albert.' Elizabeth winced at her aunt's callous words. Lady Bedlington

31

continued, 'Albert has been in a sanatorium for many years. Completely out of his mind. His young wife was so distraught, she took her own life.'

'Albert Sanderson's wife, you mean?'

'Yes, that is what I meant. Pay attention! My husband, Lord Bedlington, knew the family well. His daughter from his first marriage ... you remember my step-daughter Cassandra?' Elizabeth nodded, vaguely remembering a pale, slender woman with sad eyes. 'She was in love with Albert Sanderson and they planned to marry, but your uncle forbade it because Sanderson was so clearly beneath her. Oh she is a tiresome girl. She never comes to see me. Lives on our Devon estate in a tiny cottage, and writes books. She is an old maid now of course. Thirty-three years old. She shall never marry. That's what happens when one goes and falls for the lower classes. Men of breeding are more reluctant to offer marriage. It really was very clumsy of her.'

'So she wasn't the one who committed

suicide.' Elizabeth was getting sorely confused.

'Good Lord, no. Honestly child, you have met her, have you not? So she could hardly be dead. She may be tiresome, but Bedlingtons are made of stronger stock than that! It was Lucinda, Albert Sanderson's young bride, who took her own life.'

'Lucinda! Mr. Sanderson said that name. He said he'd seen her.'

'Nonsense. He can't have. She's dead. Now, can we please stop talking about such distressing subjects? Ah, Doctor Wheston, you've arrived.'

Elizabeth spun around to see Doctor Wheston and his friend, Liam Doubleday. She wondered how long they had been standing at the boudoir door.

'Miss Dearheart,' said Liam Doubleday, nodding his head in her direction. She bowed her own head and blushed a little.

'Who is this?' asked Lady Bedlington.

'This is my friend and colleague, Doctor Doubleday,' said Doctor Wheston. 'I hope

33

you don't mind me asking him to accompany me, Lady Bedlington, but he has a special interest in cases like yours.'

'What I have is incurable,' said Lady Bedlington. 'Doctors before you have tried and they have all failed to find the reason for my malady.'

'I have no doubt you're right,' said Liam. 'You are beyond medical help.' There was something in the wry way he said it and the slight curve at the corners of his mouth that made Elizabeth want to laugh.

'Well I am not in the mood to be poked and prodded by a stranger, Doctor Doubleday. I have had quite enough facing interrogation by my great niece this morning. Elizabeth, take Doctor Doubleday to the kitchen and offer him a hot drink, whilst Doctor Wheston and I attend to our business.'

'Very well, Aunt Arabella.' Elizabeth looked at Liam apologetically, but it was clear he found her aunt amusing rather than offensive. She went to the door, and as she opened it her aunt called out:

'You need not return to see me, Elizabeth. However, you may invite those prattling sisters to dinner at Bedlington Hall on Monday evening. Your father and brother too. Tell the constable I expect his presence.' Given what Lady Bedlington had said about having policemen in the house, Elizabeth was surprised, but she did not argue. Her aunt was known to be capricious. 'Doctor Wheston,' said Lady Bedlington, 'you, your wife and your colleague will join us.'

The invitations were couched as a command rather than a request. Elizabeth began to suspect that like the sisters, her aunt had become enthralled with the recent murder and wanted to know more details. Especially as it now seemed she had known the man. 'I believe you attended the murdered man yesterday, Doctor Wheston. You can tell me all about it on Monday night. At this moment in time I am more concerned about my own health.'

Elizabeth led Liam Doubleday down

to the kitchen. The servants were about other business, which meant they had the kitchen to themselves. He took a seat at the large table, whilst she boiled water for the coffee. 'You must forgive my aunt,' she started to say.

'You have not need to apologise, Miss Dearheart. I have met enough women like your aunt in the past to know how to deal with difficult personalities.'

Despite the fact that his words were true, Elizabeth felt a sudden surge of loyalty to her aunt. 'She has had to contend with much illness,' she said. 'Genuine illness, I mean. She had pneumonia at the age of fifteen, from which her lungs have never truly recovered.'

'And they never will if she insists on lying in bed all day,' said Liam.

'I suppose you suggest vigorous walks, Doctor Doubleday.'

'I suggest she at least walks as far as the drawing room and garden every day. I can hardly understand why she wants an orangery if she is not going to enjoy the benefit of it.'

Elizabeth looked at him sharply. Just how long had he and Doctor Wheston been listening? They must have entered the house only a few moments after she did.

'I must confess, Miss Dearheart,' said Liam, smiling, 'that when I saw you walking towards Bedlington Hall and learned that John Wheston was visiting today, I asked to accompany him. So that I could see you again.' He looked abashed. 'And now I have offended you. Let's not talk of your aunt. Let's talk of Midchester. Tell me about it. About its people.'

'There's not much to tell, Doctor Doubleday.'

'Please, call me Liam.'

'One thing I can tell you about Midchester is that one is seldom on first name terms with someone they only met a couple of days ago.'

'Oh, yes, merry old England, where neighbours wait ten years before saying good morning. But, I must admit, I'm glad to hear it, as I rather like calling you Miss Dearheart.' He curled the word around his tongue in a way that was very sensual.

'Would you like cream in your coffee?' Elizabeth wondered why it seemed she was offering him so much more.

'No, thank you.'

'Sugar?'

He shook his head, murmuring his thanks as she passed a steaming cup of black coffee to him. 'You were telling me about Midchester.'

'It is a quiet town. Nothing ever happens here. Or at least, it didn't until the other day. The trouble with nothing ever happening is that people have plenty of time to make things up. Reputations have been ruined through gossip, when people have nothing better to do.'

'Yes, I know what you mean,' he said darkly. 'Talk can cost lives.' He appeared to be lost in some thoughts of his own.

'But the people here are good people,' Elizabeth said quickly. She wondered why she felt the need to defend every-thing to him. Perhaps, she thought, it was because Midchester was so much a part of her, and a slight against Midchester felt like a slight against her. And yet had she not longed to leave it, to seek out adventure elsewhere?

'I'm sure they are, Miss Dearheart.' He took a sip of coffee. 'This is wonderful. So few English people know how to make good coffee.'

'You've travelled then, Doctor Double-day?'

'I left Ireland as a teenager, and have never returned. Tell me, do you know this Lucinda of whom the dead man spoke?'

'No, as I already told you, there is no one in Midchester of that name.'

'Are you sure? In a town where no one uses first names, it's possible.'

'But one knows anyway,' said Elizabeth. 'I don't know how we know, but we do. Anyway, it now seems that the poor man probably just saw someone who looked like his dead sister-in-law.'

'Yet he was murdered, and he spoke her name as if it were important.'

'He was delirious, I should think. They do say that sometimes when a person is dying, they see their life flashing before them.' Elizabeth struggled to convince herself, for she too thought the name of Lucinda was important in some way. She could not help wondering why Liam Doubleday was so interested.

She looked at him closely for the first time. He was very handsome, and had the last vestiges of a tan, which left him with a slightly pale and wan look. His eyes were deep, almost violet blue, rimmed with thick dark lashes. He had taken his hat off to reveal that whilst his short hair was black, there were fine silver streaks running through it. She wondered if she had misjudged his age, and that perhaps he was older. But his face was that of a young man. Something had sent him prematurely grey. Not that it was unattractive. The hint of silver gave him a distinguished air.

He had arrived in Midchester from nowhere, the only other stranger in town apart from the dead man. And he had been in the vicinity of the pond. On the other hand, Doctor Wheston knew him, and Doubleday would hardly be likely to make himself known to his old friend, or even to be near the victim as he lay dying and still capable of speech, if he had killed Sanderson. Assuming it *was* Sanderson.

There was definitely something mysterious about Liam Doubleday. She tried to remember something else that had seemed odd to her at the time, but it floated just out of her reach, before bursting like a lone balloon.

After Doctor Wheston had finished treating her aunt, and taken some coffee himself, Elizabeth said farewell to the two men at the gates of Bedlington Hall. She made her way to Constable Hounds's house, where she informed him about the possible identity of the dead man. The constable lived in a small cottage on the edge of the village. Given the lack of any real crime in Midchester, Hounds earned his real living as a blacksmith. His forge was next door to the cottage.

'Yes, I reckon you're right, Miss Dearheart,' said Hounds. 'I shouldn't need to bother Her Ladyship over this. My own investigations point to it being Sanderson. A gentleman by that name had booked into the Bear Inn on Friday night, I reckon to go and see your aunt. He has not returned since Sunday morning, when he mentioned to the landlord that he had to go out and meet someone. He left all his stuff there. The landlord is out today, visiting the brewery, but when he returns I'll ask him to identify the dead man. That's not all. There's more news, which will solve the case for us.'

'What news?' asked Elizabeth.

'His brother, Albert Sanderson, has been in a mental institution for some time. He escaped a few months ago and is still at large. So it is likely that Mr. Sanderson died at the hands of his own brother.'

'How does that follow?' asked Elizabeth.

'His brother is a madman, and on the

42

run from a madhouse to which our victim sent him. Surely that is enough evidence.'

'Just because his brother has mental problems, that does not make him a murderer,' said Elizabeth.

'Well that's where you're wrong, Miss Dearheart. You see, there are rumours that Mr. Albert Sanderson murdered one of his clients to get the man's money. That's why he ended up in the institution.'

'My aunt never mentioned that.'

'She happen doesn't know. It was all hushed up. They've got money, you see. Rich people can easily avoid scandal. But everyone knew he'd done it. Scotland Yard is sending me a picture of him. Meanwhile, I will have to put up a poster with a description.'

'But if the Sandersons had money, why would Albert need to steal it from a client?'

'Men get greedy, Miss. And he's not quite right in the head.'

'What does he look like?' asked Elizabeth. 'So we can all be on the lookout for him.'

Hounds read from the sheet of paper in front of him. 'He's thirty-five years old, about six feet tall. Got blue eyes and dark hair.'

'What?' Elizabeth felt the room sway around her.

'Are you all right, Miss?'

'Yes, I'm just a little . . . isn't it strange, how normal his description seems? He could be anyone, couldn't he?'

'Yes, that's true. Be on your guard, Miss Dearheart. Madmen can seem very sane when they want to be.'

3

Elizabeth knew that she should tell Constable Hounds about Liam Doubleday. He was a stranger to Midchester, and it seemed to her that it was quite possible that Doctor Wheston was not really a friend, but had treated Liam in a medical capacity. But if that were the case, and Liam was the escaped man, why was Doctor Wheston introducing him as a colleague? Unless Wheston was afraid of something. Surely if Liam was on the run from the madhouse, he would not risk being seen in public.

She thought again about the moment the two men had met near the pond. What had Liam said? Something about 'I bet you're surprised to see your old friend, Liam Doubleday'. Something about that greeting niggled her, but she could not put her finger on it.

Silently chastising herself for being

nearly as obsessed with crime as Miss Graves and Mrs. Chatterbucks, she said good day to Constable Hounds and returned home. On the way she met Mr. Hardacre. He strode through the village, looking every inch the local squire, and drawing admiring glances from the ladies who were out doing their Christmas shopping.

'Good day, Miss Dearheart.' He raised his hat.

'Good day, Mr. Hardacre. How is Miss Hardacre this morning?'

'She is well, and will soon be able to leave the house. In fact she is thinking of taking a walk this afternoon if the weather picks up. She does love the snow.'

'If it is not an imposition, perhaps I could join her,' said Elizabeth. 'I have missed her company these past couple of days.'

'I am sure she will be delighted. I may even come with you both.'

'That would be lovely. And perhaps as well, with a madman on the loose.'

'What is that you say about a madman?'

Elizabeth explained what Constable Hounds had told her about Albert Sanderson. 'Perhaps I am not supposed to say,' she said, 'as he has not made it common knowledge yet. But I am sure I can trust you with the information.'

'Well, I hope they catch this madman soon. It is a sad day in England when a man out walking can be struck down and left in such dire circumstances,' said Hardacre. 'Perhaps I should walk you home, Miss Dearheart.'

Elizabeth laughed. 'Thank you, but I hardly think anything will befall me at this time of day.' She forgot that Mr. Sanderson had died on Sunday morning.

'Still, we must all take care of Midchester's favourite daughter.' He bowed as he said it, whilst Elizabeth's already rosy cheeks burned a little redder.

She composed herself and walked away, saying, 'I shall be perfectly all right, Mr. Hardacre. Please, tell your dear sister I will call on her after luncheon.' It seemed odd to her, but a week before she might have been thrilled by the offer of Mr. Hardacre walking her home. Now she was surprised with how little she cared.

★ ★ ★

Elizabeth returned home and ate lunch with her father and brother, then once again set out. Samuel walked part of the way with her. 'I'm going to look for clues,' he said. She had not had a chance to tell her father about Albert Sanderson, as she did not want to speak in front of Samuel. It would not do for to frighten a child with such details.

'Dearest, I wish you would not. Leave it to Constable Hounds to deal with. You may get into difficulties.'

'Oh I shall be alright, Lizzie,' Samuel said airily. 'I'm going to call on Johnny Fletcher and ask if he'll go with me.'

Thinking there was safety in numbers, Elizabeth agreed. Johnny Fletcher was the eleven-year-old-son of the local magistrate. As the only boy in Midchester near to Samuel's age, Johnny and Samuel spent a lot of time playing together. This would be an adventure for them, and tire Samuel out nicely for bedtime. She doubted the boys would find anything very important. The falling snow would have destroyed much of the evidence, including any footprints.

'Just be careful near to the pond, Samuel,' she warned him. 'It looks frozen solid, but the ice can easily crack.'

'Yes, all right,' said Samuel in singsong tones. 'I'm going to call for Johnny first anyway, so we shall be together.'

She waved to her brother and continued towards the manor house that Mr. Hardacre and his sister rented. It was on the other side of the copse. It could be reached by the main Midchester road, but it was much easier to go around the edge of the pond, which cut off an entire corner of the woods and an adjacent field.

She was about one hundred yards from the pond when Liam Doubleday approached her at great speed. 'Did you see her?' he asked, his eyes wild. 'Did you see her?'

'See who?' asked Elizabeth. She looked towards the pond and the surrounding area, and saw nothing but snow and ice.

'She was here. I saw her.' He gripped Elizabeth's shoulders. 'Tell me you saw her too.'

'No, I saw no one. Only you.' And that scared Elizabeth, because he was quite clearly in a deranged state, but there was no one to help her if he turned murderous.

Liam calmed down immediately, leaving Elizabeth feeling even more unsettled. For was that not the mark of a madman? A sudden change from insanity to sanity? 'I apologise for frightening you like that, Miss Dearheart.'

'You looked as if you'd seen a ghost,' said Elizabeth, struggling to keep her voice even. It was said that one should not upset a madman, but humour him as much as possible.

'Perhaps she was, except . . . '

'Mr. Sanderson saw the same ghost,' said Elizabeth. He did not answer that. 'I sometimes think I see my mother,' she said. 'In the crowds during market day. It can be quite alarming. Especially when the person turns around and looks nothing like my mother. Then I'm torn between relief that my mother has not returned as a haunted spirit . . . and sadness that she has not come back to me.'

'There are no crowds here to facilitate that mistake, Miss Dearheart.'

'No, of course not. It is just hard, if we lose someone we love . . . sometimes we think we see them everywhere. In crowds; on a distant hill.' And, she supposed, if one was a murderer, the likelihood of being haunted for the rest of one's life was stronger. Not that she said that to him.

'Love?' To her surprise, he laughed bitterly. 'Yes, I suppose one can start off that way. In love. But that soon changes when one realises one has staked one's heart on a snake in the grass.' He immediately seemed shocked by his own words. 'I apologise, Miss Dearheart. I did not mean to burden you with my own nightmares. You are so . . . so fresh and sweet. It's easy to see you've never known darkness.'

'I have already told you that I've lost my mother,' said Elizabeth. She wanted to tell him that whilst Midchester might seem a quiet, a safe place to live, tragedies still happened. People lived, loved and died in much the way they did elsewhere in the world, and every family had known the pain of grief at some time. But in Midchester people survived the ache of death and disease, mainly because they had to. Life in a rural community which relied on the seasons to survive was sometimes hard, and you either toughened up, or caved in and let the darkness take you.

'Yes, you did, and I am sorry for you. But you are loved, are you not? By your father and brother. And by the people here in Midchester. Or so John Wheston tells me. Hold onto that love,

Miss Dearheart. Be happy with your lot and don't try to aim for more than you already have. By the time you realise that the love you have now is the only thing worth having, it will be too late. You will already have lost everything.'

As Elizabeth watched him walk away, she frowned. His voice had been laden with pain and anguish. It would be the right thing to tell the constable about him, but her heart and the deep sense of sympathy she felt for Liam stopped her. She almost began to tell herself that if he had murdered his client, then he must have had good reason. Her innate common sense soon overtook that opinion. She knew that there could be no excuse for taking another person's life.

No, what unnerved her about Liam Doubleday was that he appeared to have seen into her soul. He had sensed her longing to escape Midchester, even whilst she was tied to it by the bonds of love and duty. And why should she not escape, she asked herself as she walked to the Hardacres' house. Why should she not know excitement and adventure? She was all too aware that her gender answered that question. Women in the eighteen hundreds did not have the option of living adventurous lives. She supposed some did, but that came at a price: the loss of reputation and, in many cases, the loss of family. Perhaps that was what he had meant.

Sighing, she put all the dark thoughts out of her head and, despite the snow, walked with a little more vigour. As she neared the Hardacres', she saw a figure in the distance. It was a woman standing at the Midchester milestone, as if waiting for the coach, but she had no baggage. Could this be the Lucinda that Liam and Mr. Sanderson saw?

As she grew nearer, the woman turned, as if she had sensed Elizabeth's presence.

'Lady Clarissa?' said Elizabeth.

'Miss Dearheart, is it not?'

'Yes. I had no idea you were expected in Midchester.'

'Nor had I,' said Lady Clarissa Bedlington mysteriously. Despite being in her mid-thirties, she was still a very attractive woman. Not beautiful, but striking. Her grey eyes had always seemed to Elizabeth to be rather sad — reminiscent of a cloudy day, even when the sun shone.

'Are you waiting for the coach?' asked Elizabeth, simply for something to say.

'No . . . no. I came here in the hopes of finding someone . . . it's odd but I thought I saw someone I knew in the distance. Only, when I approached them, they disappeared amongst the trees. But it couldn't have been . . . '

'Who might that be?' Elizabeth believed she already knew the answer, but asked the question anyway. For some reason it made her heart ache to think of it.

'It is of no matter. I suppose I had better go and arrange some lodgings at the inn.'

'You are not staying with my aunt

. . . your stepmother?'

Lady Clarissa's lips curled. 'I can think of nothing I would like less.' She paused for a moment. 'Forgive me, Miss Dearheart. I forget that you are my stepmother's kin. You have so much kindness within you, is hard to remember the same blood flows through your veins.'

'I am sorry you are so unhappy,' said Elizabeth. It seemed the only thing she could say to a woman who looked as though her world had fallen apart. 'Perhaps you would like to stay with us. Our home is perhaps not what you are used to, but I am sure Father would be glad to welcome you.' It occurred to Elizabeth that she was overstepping many class boundaries in asking, but there was something so lost and lonely about Lady Clarissa that for the moment, none of that seemed to matter.

Clarissa appeared to think about it for a moment, before shaking her head. 'Thank you. It is a kind and gracious offer. But there are some things in which I would not want to involve you.'

'Did you know that Mr. Sanderson was dead?' The words were out before Elizabeth could stop herself.

At those words, it seemed that Clarissa's legs buckled beneath her. Elizabeth stepped forward to catch her arm, and within seconds Clarissa regained her equilibrium. 'Mr. Sanderson?'

'Mr. George Sanderson,' said Elizabeth, remembering Lady Clarissa's asociation with the dead man's brother. 'Albert Sanderson's brother.'

'When did this happen?' Clarissa composed herself, her initial shock having passed.

Elizabeth explained as tactfully as she could the details surrounding George Sanderson's death, but left out the part about the ghost of Lucinda.

'He was a kind, sympathetic man,' said Clarissa. 'I am sorry that he has died in such a dreadful way.'

'Did you know also,' said Elizabeth, watching Clarissa closely, 'that his brother has escaped from the . . . ' She almost said 'madhouse', but out of deference for Lady Clarissa's feelings changed it at the last moment to 'sanatorium'.

'I suppose that Constable Hounds has already decided that he must be guilty of his brother's murder?' Clarissa sounded bitter but not at all surprised by the news.

'Yes, I am afraid that is the case.'

'Bertie would never hurt anyone, regardless of what they say,' said Clarissa. 'That vixen bewitched him, and then treated him abominably, but he would not have killed anyone. He was . . . troubled . . . but that does not make him a killer, or responsible for her death. She deserved to die.'

Elizabeth was shocked by such language. Albert Sanderson must have a strange power over women — because he was handsome and had that hint of darkness behind his eyes — if they were willing to defend him even when he had killed. She vowed to arm herself against such feelings. She did not want to be like Lady Clarissa in fifteen years' time — bitter and unhappy over a man whom she would no doubt be sensible to avoid.

'I am just going to visit the Hardacres,' said Elizabeth. 'But if you would like to stay with us I can return home and make the arrangements.'

'Thank you, but no, Miss Dearheart. You are a good, kind soul. Unfortunately some journeys are meant to be taken alone.'

Wondering exactly what Lady Clarissa meant by that, Elizabeth went on to the Hardacres' rented manor house. Mr. Hardacre had bad news for her.

'I am afraid my sister has taken a turn for the worse, Miss Dearheart. She is unable to go walking after all and has gone back to bed. But she is eager to see you and hear all the gossip. Would it be too much trouble for you to sit with her for a while, so that I can attend to the household accounts?'

'Not at all. I would be delighted to.'

'You are an angel sent from above.

One day perhaps I won't have to deal with those awful accounts alone. My dream is that I will find my own angel to help me.' His words were so full of meaning that Elizabeth blushed. Yet something about Mr. Hardacre had changed. Elizabeth did not know what. He was as handsome and attentive as ever. Yet the attraction she previously felt towards him had dimmed. When she looked at him, all she could see was Liam Doubleday. She began to wonder if madness was indeed infectious, as many people feared.

When she entered Dora Hardacre's boudoir, she was struck by the difference between that and Lady Bedlington's. Whereas her great aunt's room was dark and dreary, Dora's room, though dark because of the weather, was cosy. A big fire burned in the grate, and candles lit up the dark corners.

Dora lay back on a chaise-longue, dressed in a luscious red velvet housecoat. She was about thirty-two years old. Large cornflower blue eyes, golden hair and rounded cheeks made her look years younger. She really was the prettiest woman Elizabeth had ever seen.

'Miss Dearheart, how kind of you to come,' said Dora. She pulled herself up to a sitting position. 'I do apologise. I was so looking forward to our walk.'

'Please, there is nothing to apologise for,' said Elizabeth. She reached out and took Dora's hand. 'Oh, you're freezing cold. Can I get you anything? A hot water bottle, or a warm drink?'

'No, I will be fine. It is bad circulation. I am sure that if I could get up and about I would be much better, but sadly my brother insists I rest. He is the kindest, most attentive brother one could have.' Dora smiled, showing dimpled cheeks. 'And he is most taken with you.' Her already large eyes widened and were filled with laughter. 'All day, he sings your praises. If I were not so taken with you myself, I should be most jealous of all the attention he pays you.'

Not for the first time that day, Elizabeth felt herself blushing. 'I am sure that is not so,' she said. 'I'm such a dull little thing.'

'I'll let you in on a secret. My brother has travelled the world in search of adventure, but what he really wants is to settle in a place like Midchester, in a tiny cottage, with a pretty wife.'

'Have you both travelled widely?' asked Elizabeth. 'Do tell me about it. I would love to travel.'

'We have seen the world — America, China, India, Africa. But there is no place like home, as I'm sure you know, and Midchester would be a wonderful place to settle. If only my brother were not forced to earn a living . . . '

Despite her admiration for Dora Hardacre, Elizabeth felt herself bristle. Why did people keep urging her not to seek excitement and adventure? Especially when they themselves had travelled widely. Were the wonders of the world some secret they wished to keep to themselves? Did she have to join a special club in order to be deemed suitable? Every time she mentioned the world outside Midchester, she was reminded of the town's virtues. It was most irritating.

She suddenly realised that Dora had been talking during her reverie. 'I'm sorry, Miss Hardacre, I was miles away.' Or at least I wish I was, she thought.

'I was saying if my brother were not forced to earn a living, we could stay. It is outrageous that a gentleman of his standing must get his hands dirty — albeit in an office rather than in a coalmine — but there it is. I would help, but I am a mere woman, and have no skills. So our choices are made for us . . . '

'You're leaving Midchester?'

'Yes, my brother's business interests are calling him elsewhere.'

'Oh no,' said Elizabeth. 'We will be sorry to lose you.'

'Well, it does not have to happen yet. Now, you must tell me all about this murder. How exciting it must have been for you to be 'at the scene of the crime' as they say.'

Elizabeth hesitated to use the word 'exciting' for fear it might make her sound like the sisters, but she had to admit that the murder had brought a strange sense of adventure into her life. Perhaps all that awaited her in Midchester was the chance of turning into Mrs. Chatterbucks or Miss Graves, revelling in others' misfortune. She shuddered at the thought, remembering with shame how she had said things to Lady Clarissa, just to gauge her reaction. In the end, she comforted herself in the knowledge that all she had was a healthy interest in finding the guilty.

4

Mrs. Chatterbucks and Miss Graves were right in that Lady Bedlington knew how to keep a good table, but it was the first time they had been allowed to see it. Despite her earlier impatience, Elizabeth felt a strange affection for them, as they sat amidst the candlelight with a table that groaned with more food than they would see in a month.

Dressed in black lace gowns that had been fashionable some thirty years previously, the sisters were initially on their best behaviour, mindful of the fact they were in the presence of a great personality. Lady Bedlington, also dressed in black lace, but in a gown recently ordered from Paris, sat in a bath chair at the head of the table, smiling benignly at the other guests. She reminded Elizabeth of an aged panther waiting to pounce. The guests, apart from the sisters, were Elizabeth's father, Doctor and Mrs. Wheston, Constable Hounds, the magistrate, Mr. Jenkins and his wife, and Mr. Hardacre; and perusing the scene, with an air of detached amusement, was Liam Doubleday.

Seeing Hardacre and Doubleday in the same room together, it was hard for Elizabeth to decide who was the most attractive. They each had their own charm; but whereas Hardacre was the typical English gentleman, with fine whiskers and a proud bearing, Doubleday had a wilder air altogether. It was not that he lacked proper manners. Far from it. He was clearly a gentleman, and most charming to everyone; but like her aunt's panther-like stance, there was a sense that Liam Doubleday might just pounce. His eyes were like flames directed at her heart. Was it that same fire in Liam's eyes that attracted the otherwise cold Lady Clarissa?

'Tell me, Constable,' said Lady Bedlington. 'Are you any closer to catching the man's killer?'

'I ham hafraid not, Your Grace,' said Hounds, sounding quite unlike Elizabeth had ever heard him. Her heart went out to him, and she wished he could relax a little in her aunt's presence.

'I'm a lady, not a duchess, though the mistake is forgivable. After all, if I had not settled for Lord Bedlington and this dreadful pile,' she looked around the dining room, which would hold the constable's cottage twice with room to spare, 'I might have married the Duke of Devonshire. Go on.'

'We har, hof course, trying to track down 'is brother, Halbert Sanderson.'

'Halibut?'

'Albert,' Elizabeth offered, to save Hounds from any more embarrassment. She noticed Liam looking at her, then at Hounds. His eyes were still amused, but they held something else. She took it to be the same sympathy she felt for the constable. 'But,' Elizabeth continued, 'I don't believe that just because a man suffers from a nervous disease it automatically makes him a killer. I hear that his brother, Mr. George Sanderson, was a kind, gentle man, who did his best to help Albert during his troubles.'

'Even a good dog will bite you eventually,' said Lady Bedlington sagely.

'Oh yes,' said Miss Graves, fortified by a glass of wine. 'Remember that old collie, Hector, we had as children — Georgiana? It bit the stable boy, and the poor lad had to have his leg chopped off. It proves that in the midst of life we are in death.'

'But surely it was only the stable boy's leg that died,' said Liam. Elizabeth almost choked on her wine.

'Well, funnily enough,' said Mrs. Chatterbucks, 'he did insist on giving it a full Christian burial. Said he didn't want to be without it when he got to heaven. Then there was the time that the butler got bitten by our Labrador. Took the end of his finger off. Had to be put down.'

Elizabeth suspected the stories were less about the butler's misfortune and more about Mrs. Chatterbucks wanting

Lady Bedlington to know that they, too, had come from landed gentry. The sisters had been the youngest siblings of three older sisters and two older brothers, all of whom died before they were thirty. It was hardly surprising that they had such a fixation with death. By the time it came the turn to make their entrance into society, the estate had been entailed away to a male cousin who had no intention of doing the decent thing by marrying one of them.

'The butler had to be put down?' said Doctor Wheston. Mrs. Wheston exchanged glances with Elizabeth, then stared resolutely at her food, whilst struggling to keep her face straight.

'No, the dog, of course.'

'That is a relief,' said Lady Bedlington. 'It is hard enough to get a decent butler.'

'I do hope the butler's finger was given a decent burial,' said Liam. Elizabeth dare not catch his eye.

'Well in a manner of speaking,' said Miss Graves. 'It was inside the dog, you see.'

'Anyway, back to the recent murder,' said the Reverend Dearheart, as the guests began to splutter into their soup. 'It is a sad day for Midchester when a man loses his life. Having said that, I have never seen the town so invigorated.'

'Really, Philip, one would think you approve,' said Lady Bedlington. 'Of course, when one marries beneath one's class . . . '

'One is happier than one has ever been in one's life,' said Philip Dearheart firmly, smiling at his daughter. 'Surely as a possible consort for a duke who gave him up to marry a mere lord you would understand that, Arabella.'

Lady Bedlington scowled at the reverend, and then pointedly started talking about other matters.

'I like your father very much, Miss Dearheart,' said Liam later, when the men had joined the women in the drawing room for after-dinner coffee. She stood by the window, looking out at the falling snow, letting the draught through

70

the panes cool her flushed cheeks. The fact that he stood so close to her did not help.

'I'm really rather fond of him myself,' said Elizabeth. Liam did not know it, but he had just paid her the highest compliment he could.

'And have you inherited his fearlessness?'

'Oh no, I'm afraid of everything.'

'I don't believe that. There's been a murder, talk of ghosts, people seeing things that aren't there, and yet you still stride through Midchester, helping others, and bringing light in the darkness.'

'I suppose I believe, perhaps a trifle arrogantly, that Midchester belongs to me, and I refuse to let any murderers or ghosts steal it from me. Besides, most murderers only kill once. Whatever the reason poor Mr. Sanderson was struck down, I think that reason probably died with him. Don't you?' She looked at him intently, trying to read his mind.

'I hope so, Miss Dearheart. I . . . I would hate to see any more trouble brought to this wonderful town of yours. Midchester is like a haven in the storm. All around us there is an industrial revolution taking place — railways, factories, and one day they say man will take to the skies. Yet this town remains oblivious to all that.'

'And you think that's a good thing, refusing to move with the times?'

'I always think it's better to let the times come to you, Miss Dearheart, rather than to chase after them. I did too much of that. I wanted to be a pioneering doctor. I travelled the world in pursuit of that, learning from the best. But do you know what being a real doctor is?'

'What?'

'It's doing what John Wheston does. Sitting at peoples' bedsides, listening to their worries, assuring them they're going to pull through. A man loses that when he chases after the glittering prizes. He forgets that there are human beings at the end of those pioneering treatments.'

'But surely if there were no pioneering treatments, they would not have found the cure for smallpox.'

'It wasn't the medical men who found that cure, Miss Dearheart. Oh they took credit for it. But it was the milkmaids and dairy farmers who first discovered it. Simply by being among cows that had cowpox and realising that unlike their neighbours, they were free from the disease. It is that quiet discovery, a realisation formed over decades, which really matters. Not the big 'let's rush this through and make a lot of money out of it' discoveries of the men of science.'

Elizabeth felt confused. As far as she was aware, Albert Sanderson had no medical training, yet Liam spoke like a man who knew what he was talking about. On the other hand, she had learned about the discovery of the smallpox vaccine by reading books and newspapers. Was it not just as likely that Albert Sanderson had read the same books? Or even more likely that being in a sanatorium would put him in the way of much medical talk?

'It is a pity that Lady Clarissa could not join us,' said Elizabeth, watching him closely.

'Lady Clarissa?'

'My aunt's step-daughter.'

'What?' Lady Bedlington's voice rang out imperiously across the room. She was involved in a game of bridge with the sisters and Mr. Jenkins. 'What was that about Clarissa?'

'I said it was a shame she could not be here.'

'She's down on our estate in Devonshire, I should imagine.'

'Oh no,' said Mrs. Chatterbucks, who sat by the fire, her eyes gleaming, either from the heat or the glass of port she had just finished. 'I saw her in town only this morning. She is staying at the Blue Peacock Inn, I believe.'

'Why has no one told me this? Really,' said Lady Bedlington, 'it is coming to something when a girl does not come to see her dear step-mama.'

Though it was well known that Lady Clarissa and Lady Bedlington had never been dear to each other, no one contradicted Her Ladyship.

'Is it true that she was once engaged to the dead man's brother?' asked Mr. Jenkins.

'Yes, many years ago,' said Lady Bedlington. 'It was a bad match, and my dear husband would not permit it.'

'It's sad when two people who should be together are kept apart,' said the reverend.

'Nonsense Philip. It was just as well. He drove his wife to suicide.'

'What is it with these dreadful men?' asked Miss Graves, her eyes shining in the candlelight. 'First the Sanderson man, and now the Demon Doctor of Delhi.'

'The Demon Doctor of Delhi?' said Mr. Hardacre. He had been very quiet all evening, though Elizabeth had been aware of him watching her as she talked to Liam. 'What is that all about?'

'Oh, did you not see the newspaper?'

said Miss Graves. 'A Doctor Bradbourne based in India. Embezzled money from a rich patient, then killed the poor man. Then Mrs. Bradbourne took her own life. They never found her body, so they think she was probably eaten by a crocodile.'

'That is unlikely,' said Liam. 'There are no crocodiles in the Ganges. There are only gharials, which are much smaller, albeit similar creatures. But they're not man-eaters.'

'You seem to know a lot about it, Doctor Doubleday,' said Mr. Hardacre. Liam did not answer.

The atmosphere became thicker, but Elizabeth could not put her finger on why.

'Men are beasts,' said Mrs. Chatterbucks. 'Of course, my Herbert was not. Goodness, he was asleep by eight o'clock most evenings.' Elizabeth detected a hint of disappointment.

'Yes, I always found a sleeping draught useful for that,' said Lady Bedlington, 'in his lordship's cocoa. It dispenses with most night-time unpleasantness where men are concerned.'

'Does it?' said Mrs. Chatterbucks. 'Well, I'm sure I never gave Herbert a sleeping draught.'

'No, but I'll hazard a guess he took a few himself,' muttered Constable Hounds, who was standing near to Elizabeth.

'What was that, Constable?'

'I said, I'd better be getting myself off. With your leave, Lady Bedlington.' Elizabeth was glad to see that the constable had dispensed with his earlier attempts at speaking in what he believed was an upper-class accent.

'No, not yet. We were interrupted at dinner. All the talk of legs and dogs.' She cast a murderous glance at the sisters. Luckily they were so overwhelmed to be breathing the same air as Her Ladyship they did not notice the insult. 'I believe Sanderson saw someone he knew in the village, did he not?'

'Yes, that's right, Your Ladyship. He did not say whom, but he told the landlord at the inn that he was going to meet someone. The landlord got the feeling it was a lady.'

'Lucinda?' said Elizabeth.

'There's no one around here of that name,' said Mrs. Chatterbucks. 'We've asked, haven't we, Henrietta?'

'Yes, indeed,' said Miss Graves. 'My sister and I have been doing a fair bit of sleuthing.'

'You really should be careful, ladies,' said the constable. 'And tell your Samuel to be careful too, Reverend. I know he and Johnny Fletcher — begging your pardon Mr. Fletcher — have been looking for clues, but it's a bit dangerous out there. Young Johnny swears he saw someone building the snowman around Mr. Sanderson, so he has been out and about looking at everyone to see if he recognises them as the man's assailant.'

'I'll have a word,' said the Reverend. 'Though one would hope this is the only murder we'll ever have in Midchester.'

'Oh, I don't know about the only one, Reverend,' said Constable Hounds.

'It was before this here young lady' — he gestured to Elizabeth — 'was born and before you took over the parish church. A man murdered his business associate. Funnily enough his young wife killed herself too. And her two children. Tragic case.'

'The children too?' said Elizabeth. 'That's dreadful.'

'Their bodies was never found,' said Constable Hounds, 'but their clothes was found near the river. Chances are they were swept into the estuary and out to sea.'

'Oh, I'd heard about that,' said Miss Graves. Her voice held a note of regret, about it being something she'd only heard about. 'What a pity it happened before most of us came here.'

'Let me see,' said Mrs. Chatterbucks. 'They said she was quite a common thing. Not well-born at all. But had a way with her. What was her name?'

'Lucinda Hargreaves,' said the constable. 'I remember because I thought about her when I heard Mr. Sanderson had said the name Lucinda.'

'Is it possible he knew her?' asked Elizabeth.

'I suppose it is. He's been doing business in this area for a long time.'

'Then he could have seen her!' For some reason Elizabeth felt relieved. Because if it was Lucinda Hargreaves, then it was more likely she who had killed George Sanderson, not Liam — or Albert Sanderson, if that was his real name. Not that it altered the fact that Albert Sanderson — or Liam — was involved with Lady Clarissa. That tore at Elizabeth's heart. She tried to tell herself she was being stupid. She had only known Liam for just over a week, and for a lot of that time she had suspected him of murder.

Mr. Hardacre yawned. 'This is all fascinating, really, but I must get back to my sister.'

'Of course,' said Elizabeth. 'I am sorry she could not be here tonight.'

'As was she,' said Mr. Hardacre. 'Hopefully she will be able to see you all again before we leave.'

'Then it is certain you are leaving?' said Elizabeth.

'Yes.'

'But you will stay until after Christmas, I hope. Father and I had hoped to invite you both to the vicarage for Christmas luncheon.'

'Humph,' said Lady Bedlington. 'It is something when outsiders are invited before family.'

'We did invite you, Arabella,' said the reverend. 'You refused, as you always do.'

'I am quite sure you did not, but as I am not one to bear a grudge, I will come. I suppose these two will be there.' She gestured to the sisters.

'Certainly,' said Elizabeth emphatically. She had no intention of letting her aunt decide on the guest list. A glance from her father told her that he understood and approved of her decision.

'Very well, I suppose one has to make allowances.'

The sisters smiled, but Elizabeth saw

Mrs. Chatterbucks' smile waver slightly. Her aunt's insult had not gone unnoticed that time.

Mr. Hardacre left them to return home. Elizabeth noticed with some disappointment that he had not offered anyone else a ride home in his carriage. She excused him because he was no doubt anxious to get home to his sister. Any detours through the town would only delay his return.

Not long afterwards, the party broke up. Mr. Jenkins, Doctor Wheston and Mrs. Wheston went home in one carriage. Liam expressed a desire to walk. Constable Hounds said he would accompany him and take in the night air.

The sisters, Elizabeth and her father took another carriage, for which Elizabeth was grateful. Both women were rather subdued.

'You must not let my aunt upset you,' said Elizabeth. In truth she was furious with her aunt for treating their feelings in such a cavalier fashion.

'Oh, Her Ladyship was most gracious,' said Mrs. Chatterbucks. 'And I suppose ... well ... we are rather tiresome at times.'

'Please do not think so,' said Elizabeth. She had to admit to often thinking the sisters tiresome, but it did not excuse her aunt's rude behaviour. 'My aunt is rude to everyone, especially to her family. Her wealth and status allow her to get away with much that an ordinary person would not.'

'Quite,' said the reverend. 'She is a lonely woman who does not realise that if she could open her heart to others — as you both do — she would not be quite so lonely.'

'We are not lonely, because we have each other,' said Miss Graves, her eyes misty. 'And we have dear friends like you who, despite our faults, watch over us.'

'And we always will,' said Elizabeth. 'I am sure that you forgive our faults too.'

'Oh my dearest girl,' said Mrs.

Chatterbucks. 'You and the Reverend have shown us nothing but kindness.'

Elizabeth felt so sure both sisters were about to cry that she dared not say anything else.

5

During the coach ride home, Elizabeth took to thinking about what she had learned over the past few days. Mr. George Sanderson had been murdered whilst on a business trip to see her aunt. That much was certain. He had mentioned the name Lucinda, and it now transpired that some time ago, before Elizabeth was born, a woman called Lucinda Hargreaves was married to a man who murdered a business associate, after embezzling his money. Then Lucinda Hargreaves was believed to have taken her own life and those of her two young children. Elizabeth shuddered at the thought. Whatever happened with Mr. Hargreaves, and the shame Lucinda might have felt, the children were not to blame.

Into the confusing equation came the story about George Sanderson's brother

Albert, who fifteen years previously had been going to marry her aunt's step-daughter, Lady Clarissa Bedlington. He had been chased off by Lord Bedlington, and had subsequently married another girl. Then he, too, was accused of murdering a business associate, only his illness and his family connections meant he was incarcerated in a sanatorium instead. After that, his wife Lucinda was said to have taken her own life.

Could it have been the same woman? No, thought Elizabeth; that did not fit. Fifteen years previously, Elizabeth had been nine, which meant that the Lucinda from the first story — which had taken place at least ten years before that — would have been much older. Nevertheless, there were too many coincidences in the stories. What that meant, Elizabeth did not know.

To confuse her emotions even more, Liam Doubleday had come into the story quite suddenly, and at the same time as she found Mr. Sanderson's body. His greeting to his friend, which went something like, 'I warrant you're surprised to see your old friend, Liam Doubleday' ... Why had it struck Elizabeth as odd? Of course! Before Doctor Wheston could speak, Liam had rushed forward and let him know the name by which he was to be known, just in case Doctor Wheston had called him by his real name. But why had Doctor Wheston concurred? He seemed a decent, trustworthy man, not given to subterfuge; yet if Elizabeth's suspicion was correct, he was helping his friend to pretend to be someone else.

What had Liam got to do with it all? Elizabeth guessed he was around ten years her senior, making him thirty-four or thirty-five years old. Any event before she was born would have taken place before his tenth year — and maybe even before he was born, because Elizabeth did not know the exact date of the first Lucinda's story.

A suspicion started to take hold. Elizabeth did not know why she had not thought of it before! She chided herself for her stupidity. Liam could not be Albert Sanderson, because Lady Bedlington would have recognised him from their earlier acquaintance. Unless her aunt was even more blinkered than Elizabeth thought.

But he could be the son of the first Lucinda — assuming the woman did not really die and just took her children away with her. Which might mean the lady in question was in Midchester. But where? No, that did not fit either. She would no doubt be recognised. Unless . . . unless the years had not been kind to her. She would be a much older woman, probably in her fifties, maybe even older.

Elizabeth was still missing something. Something that had been said about Albert Sanderson's wife. What was it? Yes! That was it. Lady Bedlington had said he had married a young woman. No one would say that about a woman who was older than he; and had the woman been older, Elizabeth felt sure her aunt would have mentioned it as something out of the ordinary.

So it was possible there were two Lucindas: one older woman, with two children, who disappeared — presumed dead; and Albert Sanderson's tragic young wife, who apparently took her own life. In both cases, no bodies had been found.

Elizabeth came to with a start, realising that the carriage had stopped outside Mrs. Chatterbucks' and Miss Graves' garden gate. The reverend got out, showing them to the door and causing them to fluster a little. It made Elizabeth smile. Her father was still very handsome, and she could understand how his simple kindness would bring a thrill into their lives.

She watched them make steady steps through the snow to the door, then her eyes glanced over to the other side of the road. Doctor Wheston's house was lit up, and by the gaslight from above the door, she could see a figure walking along the pavement towards it. It was Liam. She felt her heart give a flip, and she wondered how a man she barely knew could engage her emotions so strongly.

The front door opened, and a figure emerged. A woman. She walked down the path and opened the gate, ready for Liam's arrival. It was Mrs. Wheston. When Liam reached her, she held out her arms and he took her into his. They held each other for a long time, before walking back to the house together arm-in-arm.

Elizabeth felt disappointment and heartbreak consume her. So that was the way it was. Whilst John Wheston was shielding his friend from whatever trouble he was in, Liam repaid him by seducing Wheston's pretty young wife.

As they closed the door, another figure stepped out of the shadows. How long he had been there, Elizabeth did not know. He was an old man — or at least seemed to be — with a shambling gait, dressed in the clothes of a tramp and yet having an altogether different bearing. He looked up at Doctor

Wheston's house as if trying to come to a decision, then appeared to change his mind before disappearing into the night.

* * *

With all the resilience of her youth, Elizabeth faced the next morning somewhat braver than she had felt on going to bed. What cared she about a man who lied about his identity and stole another man's wife? True, Liam might be handsome and charming, but that did not make him a good person. She vowed instead to start asking questions. She was given the chance to speak to her father at breakfast, due to Samuel rushing out to go evidence hunting with Johnny Fletcher.

'Do you think it's wise, Father?' she asked.

'It's daytime, Lizzie,' said the reverend. 'We can't stop children being children because of one madman's actions. Samuel has orders to be in by lunchtime, and to stay within sight of the town square.'

'He may not obey.'

'He's a good boy. He'll do as I say. All young boys should have adventure.'

'And what about young girls?' She sounded more brittle than she had intended.

'Young girls should follow their hearts too,' her father said mildly.

'It's just that I was thinking that as Samuel is going away to school next September, I might take a post as a governess. In the newspaper only this week there was a family — a young government consul and his wife — looking for a governess to care for their children in the Orient.'

'So far away? Could you not take a post that would allow you to come home and see your old father from time to time?'

'I am afraid that if I don't escape Midchester now, I might never escape,' said Elizabeth with far more passion than she had intended.

'Is that how you feel, my Lizzie? Trapped? I know it has been hard for you bringing up Samuel, but it seems to me you will only be doing what you have always done. Looking after children.'

'I don't want to be here all my life, like the sisters,' said Elizabeth, with the same passion. 'I'm not saying I shan't come home, but to have never been anywhere since the day you were born . . . ' She held out her hands, as if the thought were too big for her to articulate.

'Mrs. Chatterbucks and Miss Graves weren't born here, dearest. They're from Yorkshire originally. Mrs. Chatterbucks travelled the Far East with Mr. Chatterbucks. They only came here when he retired. Miss Graves has also travelled — to America as a schoolteacher, I believe, though I don't know much about her past. But she only came here about ten years ago, if you remember, to live with her sister after Mr. Chatterbucks died.'

'Yes, I remember now. It's funny, but I'd got it into my head that they had always been a part of Midchester. It certainly feels as if they've always been here. Father, did you know Lucinda Hargreaves? The one who was said to have murdered her husband?'

'I can't say I did. What, you're not suggesting she's returned as one of the sisters, are you?' The reverend laughed.

'Why not? It occurred to me that when strangers come into a community, we only know what they tell us about themselves.'

'Hardly, dear. Most people who come to Midchester arrive with letters from relatives or friends of existing residents. If they rent their home, they have to provide references from former landlords.'

'But these things can be forged, can they not? A letter from Lord or Colonel Something-or-other, saying someone is known to them. Or a letter might not say everything about a person. After all, no one would show an unkind reference.'

'It would soon be revealed if it were not true.'

'But who checks? Does anyone write to Lord or Colonel Such-and-such, asking if they really know that person? Don't we rather take people at their word? I mean, you're all right, because Aunt Arabella definitely knows you, and gave you the post of vicar here. But another young vicar might have arrived, saying he knew the bishop and showing false references, and it's almost certain that Aunt Arabella would not have bothered to check.'

'Don't you think you're rather mistrusting lately, Lizzie?' asked her father.

Elizabeth smiled. 'Yes, I am rather. It's just . . . Father?'

'Yes, dear?'

'When you met Mother, did you ever have any doubts? Aunt Arabella is convinced Mother married you for money.'

'Most women marry for money, dear.'

'That's a rather cynical attitude.' Elizabeth's eyes widened in shock.

'But not untrue. Women have to marry for money, simply because there are so few ways of them earning their own crust. But they also know that they have to live with a man for the rest of their lives, so they're often very careful to fall in love with someone who can provide for them. It's the hunter-gatherer thing, and there's nothing wrong with that.' He winked across the table at her. 'But in answer to your question, no I never had a moment's doubt. I was a pretty poor prospect back then. I had no income of my own, and had gone into the church because when I left the army I was not fit for anything else. Despite my poor prospects, your mother loved me better than anyone ever could. She loved you, and had she lived to see him grow, she would have loved Samuel. Money can guarantee many things — roof over your head, food in your belly — but it can't guarantee that you'll love and be loved. That's something you have to work at and earn all by yourself.

Sometimes I wish your Aunt Arabella would remember that.'

'If she ever knew.'

'Oh, she knew. She didn't turn the Duke of Devonshire down, you know. She adored him, and not just for his money and status. Sadly, he was never serious about his feelings. He had long since been promised to a girl from a better family, but he hid that from Arabella, and from others before her. It was only then that she married for money and status. Not quite as well as she'd hoped, and to a man who was not always kind to her or Lady Clarissa. Now she has her money and she has her status, but she seldom commands love — and even if she did, she would be incapable of loving in return.'

'You always see things better than I do,' said Elizabeth. 'Sometimes I feel so angry with people because of the way they are. Only last night, despite the times I've felt the sisters to be tiresome, I was angry with Aunt Arabella for being so rude to them.'

'Then tell her.'

'I couldn't!'

'Why not?'

'Because it's as you say, she has money and status. And besides, Father, if I upset her she may well take it out on you.'

'Arabella wouldn't do anything to me. And if she did, then there are other parishes. I may not have been worth much when she gave me the Midchester parish, but I fancy I've earned a few more honours with the Church of England since then.'

'Then she might take it out on Samuel. If not for her, he would not be going to school next year. That is what I try to remind myself when I am angry with her. That despite her rudeness, she is capable of kindness, even if it does not always feel like kindness. Oh I hate being dependent on others, Father. If I could just get away . . . '

'Do you hate it here so much, child?'

'No, not hate. I love Midchester. But I read so much about other places, and

I would so like to see them.'

'What if I were to rent a house near the sea come the summer? I would not be able to accompany you, because I have my duties here. But Sam could go, and . . . well you may not like this bit.'

'What?'

'The sisters could accompany you.'

'As chaperones, you mean?'

'You are a young, unmarried woman. I couldn't in all conscience leave you to live alone, Lizzie.'

'A house by the sea would be wonderful, Father.' Elizabeth smiled and kissed her father's head. 'Yes. I may write, you know. That's what some ladies do to earn a living. Not that I shall be very good at it. But I can pretend.' She stood up and almost danced out of the room, barely noticing the expression of impending loss on her father's face.

6

Elizabeth spent the rest of the morning on chores, readying the house for the Christmas festivities. Her father and Samuel had fetched a tree the day before, and it stood in the corner of the parlour, awaiting decoration. She knew that Samuel would be upset if she started without him, so instead she set about putting newspaper around the base, to catch the falling needles. As she put the papers into place, she idly read the news. Some of the papers were years old, having been stored in the attic and then forgotten about. Suddenly her eyes alighted on one particular headline from a newspaper dated five years previously.

The Strange Case of the Returning Wife, it read. There was an exciting development in the case yesterday when Mrs. Prudence Rivers, the wife of Bertram Rivers, who was believed to have taken her own life, returned and declared she was very much alive. Her husband, Bertram Rivers, had been tried and condemned for the murder of his elder brother and it was believed the shame had driven his young wife to her own death.

Mrs. Rivers, a beauty with golden locks, claims that she fled to a remote part of Scotland, where she was unaware of the murder enquiry. 'Had I known, I would most certainly have come forward,' she told our reporter. 'Bertram may not have been the kindest of husbands, but he was no murderer. I only found out he had been hanged because I happened to visit Edinburgh and saw it in the newspaper.'

Mr. Rivers' family have long since argued his innocence, and strongly refute claims that he was a brute to his pretty wife. Mr. Rivers' sister, Mrs. Flora Pertwee, insisted she had seen Mrs. Rivers whilst visiting a friend in Scotland during Mr. Rivers' incarceration.

Mrs. Rivers is expected to be able to

claim Mr. Rivers's estate, which amounts to an annuity of £100 per year.

A similar case took place in Calais several years ago, when the husband of a woman hanged for the murder of her rich uncle arrived several days after her execution. He, too, was thought to have taken his own life, but claimed he had merely been at sea for several months.

Elizabeth barely had time to think about why the story had arrested her attention when there was an almighty banging at the front door. She rushed through to the hall just as her father was running down the stairs.

'What on earth?' she said, flinging the door open. Liam Doubleday stood before her, soaked to the skin and shivering. At first she thought he held a bundle of rags in his arms, then with a scream of horror she realised it was Samuel.

'Quickly,' said Liam, darting into the house. 'Take me to a room with a good fire, and bring towels and blankets.'

Despite her horror, Elizabeth was

able to calm herself enough to do as he asked, leading him into the parlour. As she bustled around, looking for towels and blankets, she could hear her father speaking to Liam, asking questions.

'What happened?' she said, coming back with the towels. 'I've asked Abigail to boil some water,' she added.

'He fell into the pond,' said Liam. 'The ice broke. Luckily I was walking nearby, and saw him crying for help. Reverend, bring some warm brandy. It won't hurt him in this instance.'

Samuel lay on the sofa, gradually coming to as Liam spooned warm brandy into him. His teeth chattered, whilst both Liam and Elizabeth dried him with towels. She had brought her brother's nightshirt and housecoat, which they changed him into. Elizabeth covered him with blankets to keep out any further chill. The reverend put some more logs onto the fire.

'Sam, you were told about the pond, dearest,' said Elizabeth, trying to speak calmly.

'Johnny,' he said, struggling to speak because of the cold. He started to cry. 'Johnny still there.'

'What?' said Liam. He stood up. 'I swear I only saw Samuel. I'll go back and look.'

'No,' said the reverend. 'You dry off. I'll get a search party organised.'

'Get Doctor Wheston too,' said Liam. 'I'll need to change.'

'My father has some clothes that might fit you,' said Elizabeth. 'I'll go and put them out on his bed, then you can change.'

'Thank you, Elizabeth,' said Liam. She did not have time to think of the significance of him using her name, or chastise him for it. She could note only the small thrill it gave her to hear it on his lips. Her father went off in search of help.

'Sam, dearest, tell me what happened,' she said, whilst Liam was upstairs dressing. 'Why did you go on the pond?'

'We didn't, Lizzie,' said Samuel. 'We were in the copse, because Johnny said that's where he saw the man who built the snowman go. Then when we got there, we saw a man in amongst the trees. He started chasing us, so we ran, and the quickest way was across the pond. Only . . . ' Samuel began to cry. 'Johnny fell first, and I was trying to help him.'

'Who was this man, Sam? Can you describe him?'

'He was all dressed in rags. And with a hood. I didn't see his face.'

Liam came back into the parlour as Samuel finished speaking. 'There was a man dressed in rags outside Doctor Wheston's last night,' said Elizabeth.

'How do you know that?' asked Liam.

Elizabeth felt her face grow warm. 'We . . . erm . . . we shared the carriage with Mrs. Chatterbucks and Miss Graves. They live near to the Whestons. I just happened to be looking out and . . . and I saw him.'

'I saw the carriage as I arrived home, but I didn't see the man,' said Liam. The way he searched her face unnerved her, so she turned away and began folding Samuel's wet clothes.

'It was after you went inside with Mrs. Wheston,' said Elizabeth, trying to keep her voice light. 'He came out of the shadows. I assumed he was someone seeking help from Doctor Wheston, but then we left to return home so I don't know where he went next.' She felt unaccountably angry. 'I don't know what sort of world we live in when a man chases children and puts them in such danger! Samuel might have died.' Tears stung her eyes, and she was not entirely sure she only cried for Samuel's predicament.

'No, it is outrageous, I agree,' said Liam. 'But Samuel is fine, aren't you, Sam? He's a strong lad.'

'I hope Johnny is okay,' said Samuel.

Elizabeth turned around, silently chastising herself. Here she was, tearing herself apart over Liam's relationship with Mrs. Wheston, and another child was still in danger. 'I'm sure he will be, darling,' said Elizabeth, going to her brother. She sat on the edge of the sofa and stroked his head. His forehead felt hot. 'I think he's getting a fever,' she said to Liam.

Liam put his own hand on Samuel's head. 'It's probably just his body trying to reach its normal temperature. Or it could be the brandy.' He smiled. It was a wonderful smile. 'But keep an eye on him for a few days, and if he's unwell, either call me or Doctor Wheston. I'm going to go and see what I can do to help with finding young Johnny.'

'Thank you for bringing him home,' said Elizabeth, as she showed Liam to the door.

'I don't know what we'd do if we lost him.' Her voice caught in her throat.

'He's a fine young man.'

'Yes, he is.'

'I see your influence in him.'

'Do you?'

'Yes. In fact, Mrs. Chatterbucks was only telling me today what a wonderful mother you've been to him.'

'I only tried to do what my mother

would have done. Which is to love and care for him.'

'Then he's also a very lucky young man. Would that we all had such a lovely guardian angel.'

'Oh I'm sure Mrs. Wheston does her best.' The words were out before Elizabeth could stop herself.

'Mrs. Wheston? Yes, she is an angel too. John could not have asked for a better wife.'

'And is she the sort of wife you want?' asked Elizabeth.

'No. I've had one wife. I don't wish for another.' His lips became a thin line, and a deep frown creased his brow. 'Though why you should think I aim for Mrs. Wheston, I don't know.'

'You seem close.'

'Ah, I see. You saw us embrace last night?'

Elizabeth did not answer. It really was none of her business. Despite that, she wanted to ask him about his wife. Was she still alive? Had she died? Was he still in love with her? What had she done to hurt him so? For it was clear he had not come out of the marriage unscathed. The questions flew around her head.

Liam smiled again. 'I am not in the habit of stealing other men's wives. It is just that I have been able to bring Mrs. Wheston good news of her brother, whom she feared had been lost to her. She was merely grateful for that fact. I'm sure you understand that feeling, Elizabeth.'

'Yes, of course,' said Elizabeth. She looked down at her feet, wishing that she could hide somewhere in that vicinity. 'And I am grateful to you for saving Sam, really.'

'Do be sure to let me know if you would ever like to illustrate that with an embrace.'

Elizabeth's head shot up, her eyes widening. 'I hope,' she said, garncring her courage, 'that you will be satisfied with a handshake, Doctor Doubleday.' She held out her hand. He took it in his hand, which had only just begun to warm up. Instead of shaking hers, as she expected, he lifted it to his lips, kissing her fingers. His lips were warm and sensual, sending a thrill running along Elizabeth's arm, and through her whole body. It wasn't the first time her hand had been kissed, but it was the first time the kiss had promised so much more. Or left her wanting so much more.

That simple kiss unnerved and excited Elizabeth in ways she had never experienced before. Despite the rather staid attitude to sex in her times, she would be a fool not to realise that her response to him was of a sexual nature. It was then she realised the difference between Liam and Mr. Hardacre. Though handsome and charming, Mr. Hardacre had a coldness about him, whereas one look into Liam's eyes revealed a flame burning within that made Elizabeth tremble inwardly. She silently chastised herself. After all, she was a vicar's daughter. Her head should not be filled with such ideas of sensuality.

And yet . . . though only fourteen when her mother died, had she not been aware of such a relationship between her mother and father? Nothing overt or crass. The reverend and his wife were far too discreet and well-mannered for that. But occasionally Elizabeth had burst into the parlour to find them in an embrace that could only be described as passionate. Sometimes she witnessed a glance passing between them at bedtime. She blushed as, with her own sensual awakening, the implications of those embraces and glances became clear to her. She had a brief fantasy of her and Liam at the end of a long day, walking up the stairs hand-in-hand to a cosy bedroom where they . . . She put her cool hands to her face, which burned crimson. How could she be having such thoughts about a man she barely knew? Yet every inch of her body ached for such moments with him. Had he seen the longing in her eyes? She blushed even more. She would have to be more circumspect with him in future.

Samuel was sleeping when she went back to the parlour. She sat in the rocking chair, watching him, and wondering about poor Johnny Fletcher. But her thoughts kept returning to Liam Doubleday and the tingling in her fingers where he had kissed them. He disturbed her in a way no man ever had. How she had ever found Mr. Hardacre attractive, she did not know. Almost as if she had summoned him by thinking of it, Mr. Hardacre arrived at the vicarage door.

'I heard the news about poor Samuel, and have come to offer my help,' he said.

'Thank you, Mr. Hardacre,' said Elizabeth. She led him through to the parlour. 'He's sleeping now,' she said in a low voice. 'I can hardly bear to imagine what might have happened had Doctor Doubleday not found him.'

'Yes . . . ' There was something in Hardacre's tone that made Elizabeth look at him sharply.

'What is it?'

'It is only . . . Dear Miss Dearheart, I do not want to cause you any more distress than I know you have already suffered. But what do we know about this Doubleday? He arrives from nowhere, and has a knack of being in the wrong place at the wrong time. Was he not there when you found Mr. Sanderson's body? And now, when young Samuel is in danger?'

Elizabeth felt her knees weaken. 'What are you suggesting? That he did this to Samuel?'

Hardacre smiled. 'No, no of course not. I do not know what made me think of it. Jealousy perhaps.'

'Jealousy?'

'Miss Dearheart . . . Elizabeth, darling. You must know how I feel about you.' Mr. Hardacre caught her by the shoulders and pulled her nearer to him.

'Mr. Hardacre, please. It is inappropriate with my father out of the house.' It was strange how she had not felt that when Liam suggested she embrace him. Then she had only felt regret at being too shy to do so.

'Darling Elizabeth, I have to leave Midchester, but I want you to come with me. I have known more happiness in your company than at any other time. Dora knows of my feelings. She teases me about it, but I know that she would be most happy to have you in our family.'

Elizabeth stood back. Something felt wrong, and not just that Hardacre's proposal brought home to her that she had no such feelings for him. There was something desperate about the way Hardacre spoke, and she had a strong feeling that it was not due to love or passion.

'I am very grateful for your kind offer . . . '

'No, don't say no, not yet darling. Think about it. We leave on Boxing Day. Say you'll come with me.' He pulled her to him again and pressed his lips against hers.

Elizabeth was too shocked to stop him, and by the time she had regained her equilibrium and started to push him away she heard a polite cough.

'We have found Johnny,' said the reverend. He stood at the parlour door with Liam Doubleday.

'Oh,' said Elizabeth, stepping back and almost falling over. 'Is he well?'

'He is in a serious condition,' said Liam grimly. He was looking from Elizabeth to Hardacre, with darkness in his eyes that Elizabeth could not fathom. 'Doctor Wheston is attending him. I have just returned to see how Samuel is. But clearly he must be well, as I am sure Mr. Hardacre would not think of making love to you with a sick child in the same room. Good day.' Liam turned and stormed out of the house.

Hardacre left soon after, bowing to the reverend and saying to Elizabeth, 'Please think about my offer.'

'Are you going to?' asked the reverend, when he and Elizabeth sat down to afternoon tea. They took it in the parlour, so they could watch Samuel as he slept. Elizabeth kept some toast warm, in case her brother should awaken and feel hungry.

'I have no wish to marry Mr. Hardacre, Father. Tell me about Johnny Fletcher.'

Her father looked at her for a long time, then clearly decided not to press the matter. 'He was under the ice for some time. In fact, we had only just found him when Doctor Doubleday returned. We were sure we would have to give up poor Johnny for dead, but Doubleday argued otherwise. He said he had heard of people being revived some time after drowning in icy water. Something about the cold slowing down the bodily functions. Despite Wheston believing young Johnny had no chance, Doubleday insisted on trying to revive him. And it worked. Poor Johnny may lose a couple of toes to frostbite, and it may take him some time to recover his faculties, but he is alive. Thank the good Lord.' The reverend made a praying gesture.

'So . . . so Doctor Doubleday could

116

not have wanted Johnny and Samuel dead, could he, Father?'

'Whatever makes you say that, Lizzie?'

'Mr. Hardacre pointed out that Doctor Doubleday has a knack of being in the wrong place at the wrong time. He was there when I found Mr. Sanderson, and there when Sam and Johnny fell through the ice.'

'I find it hard to believe that a man who strove so hard to save that boy's life would have been the cause of Sam and Johnny's distress.'

'That's what I would like to think,' said Elizabeth. 'Father?'

'Hmm.' The reverend had just bitten into a slice of hot buttery toast. The butter dripped onto the plate, and he scooped it up with the bread. In the cosy room, with the firelight spreading warmth, it was hard for Elizabeth to believe there were dangers in the world. Yet Sam, lying on the sofa covered in blankets, reminded her that their comfortable lives had been invaded by such horrors.

'Why do people think that Arthur Sanderson embezzled from his associate, then murdered him?'

'From what Constable Hounds told me, they found proof in Sanderson's study of him having practised his associate's signature. They never did find out what happened to the money. As Sanderson was mentally unfit, he could not be brought to trial.'

'Father, there was a case in the papers five years ago. It was very similar. A man was hanged for murdering his associate, after embezzling money which was never found. The condemned man's wife disappeared too, only to return after his death and claim his estate. Don't you think that's strange?'

'Yes, it is rather.'

'I wish I could find out more about Lucinda Hargreaves.'

'I imagine the sisters will be your first point of call for all things murderous. They know about every murder trial going.'

'Will you be all right to care for

Samuel if I call on them after tea?'

'Lizzie . . . I want you to be careful, dearest. I'm not entirely sure that Sam and Johnny's forays into detecting haven't led to today's worries. I should never have let him go.' The reverend looked across at his son, his face a mask of guilt. 'I thought it was harmless enough. Who would think children would be hurt?'

'Johnny said he'd seen something,' said Elizabeth. 'But we all thought it was to make himself look important. I wonder now . . . '

'Exactly.'

Despite her father's warning, Elizabeth wrapped up warm and set out on her trip to see the sisters. She was just about to turn into their gate when Liam Doubleday stepped out of Doctor Wheston's front door.

'Miss Dearheart,' he called. 'May I speak with you for a moment?'

'Of course.' Elizabeth stopped and waited for him to cross the road.

'I owe you and your father an

apology for my behaviour earlier. It is not for me to judge your conduct, and I am sure that you would have had your brother's interests at heart at all times.'

'There is nothing to apologise for,' said Elizabeth. 'Mr. Hardacre took me by surprise. I mean, I was not expecting him to become so ardent.'

'He has asked for your hand in marriage?'

'Yes.'

'And will you accept?'

'No. I do not love him.' Why it was important that Liam know that, Elizabeth did not quite understand.

Liam's face visibly altered to become more relaxed, breaking into that wonderful smile. 'You're not in love with him.'

'No, I am not. He is a good . . . ' Elizabeth almost said decent, but something stopped her, 'man, but I realised today that I do not return his feelings. I hope I have not caused him too much pain.'

'He'll get over it, I'm sure,' said

Liam. There was something brittle about his voice.

'Are men's feelings always so fickle, Doctor Doubleday?'

'No more than women's.' Again that bitterness. She wished she could understand what made him feel that way. 'You are going to see the sisters?'

Elizabeth nodded. 'I wish to ask them something.'

'Are you still investigating Mr. Sanderson's murder?'

'Not investigating. Just trying to make sense of what happened.' Without realising why, Elizabeth found herself telling Liam about what she had read in the paper, and the link — the bloodied fabric — with Albert Sanderson's missing wife. 'I have heard it elsewhere recently,' she said.

'The Demon Doctor of Delhi,' said Liam.

'What?'

'His wife also went missing, after he was accused of murdering a patient after a similar embezzlement.'

'Of course! Yes, that was where I had read it. How strange that these things should happen in such far-flung places. England, France, India. It makes me wonder . . . but it happened with a man too. That was the one in France. So it could not be connected, could it?'

'People travel, Miss Dearheart.'

'Yes, I suppose they do. Well thank you, you have saved me a trip to see the sisters.'

'I am sure they would be most disappointed if you did not call. Let me come with you. I have failed to pay them my proper respects since I arrived.'

Elizabeth smiled. 'I cannot imagine that Mrs. Chatterbucks and Miss Graves are of any great interest to a man like yourself.'

'Then you do me a disservice, Miss Dearheart. They are characters, and if there is one thing I enjoy in life, it is the company of a character. Where else can I hear stories of amputated legs and dog-eaten fingers?'

'As a doctor I would have thought

everywhere you went.' Elizabeth could not help smiling. The earlier tension between them had gone, and they spoke as friends again.

'Ah, but not told with such naivety and a total lack of understanding of the humorous aspects.'

'You must not make fun of them,' said Elizabeth sternly, smiling despite herself. 'It is not kind.'

'No, it is not. And I would not dream of it.' His eyes twinkled.

'Miss Dearheart!' Miss Graves was calling from the sisters' front door. For a moment Elizabeth felt sad that the spell between her and Liam had been broken. 'We have been awaiting your visit. Isn't it wonderful?'

'Isn't what wonderful?' Miss Graves' words hardly seemed appropriate with two children having been harmed.

'Why, your aunt's invitation to her Christmas ball.'

'I have heard of no such occasion,' said Elizabeth.

'I daresay her footman called at your

house whilst you were on your way here,' said Mrs. Chatterbucks, pushing past her sister. 'It is on Christmas Eve. The footman said that most of the townsfolk have been invited. Well those from good families, that is.'

When Elizabeth reached home, she found out that was indeed the case. Her aunt, with uncharacteristic generosity, had decided to hold a Christmas ball at Bedlington Hall for the first time in many years.

Liam had walked her home so that he could take a proper look at Samuel. They need not have worried. Her brother was sitting up, eating toast with damson jam, and telling the reverend excitedly about his and Johnny Fletcher's adventure on the pond.

'Johnny said he saw a man in rags near to the snowman on the day we found Mr. Sanderson,' Samuel was telling his father. 'So we went out looking for him.'

'Was it the same man in rags?' asked the reverend. 'The one who chased you, I mean.'

124

Elizabeth and Liam each took a seat to listen to Samuel's story.

'I don't know, Father. Like I told Lizzie, he had his face covered in a hood,' said Samuel. 'If Doctor Doubleday had not been at the other side of the pond . . . '

'What?' said Elizabeth, her heart lightening for the first time since Samuel had been brought home.

'I saw Doctor Doubleday on the other side of the pond, didn't I, sir?'

'Yes, that's right,' said Liam. Elizabeth could tell by his expression that he knew exactly what she had thought. She cast her eyes to the floor in shame.

'And I said to Johnny, 'Come on, let's go to the doctor. He will help.' And he did.' Samuel looked up at Liam as if he were a hero of immense proportions.

'So did you see the man clearly?' Elizabeth asked Liam, wondering why he had not mentioned it before.

'No. As Sam said, he wore a hood. And I was standing much further away and only looked up when Sam shouted.

I did not even see Johnny. Only Sam. I had gone there to . . . ' Liam stopped, and Elizabeth immediately sensed he was hiding something. It gave her a sinking feeling. Even if he had not harmed the boys, he still had secrets. 'To take in the fresh air. Of course as soon as Samuel fell in, my attention was taken up with pulling him out.'

'For which we are most grateful,' said the reverend. 'If there is any way we can repay you . . . '

Liam smiled. 'If you would do me the honour of allowing me to accompany Miss Dearheart to the Christmas ball, I would consider all debts repaid.'

7

The night of the Christmas ball was made somewhat merrier by the news that Johnny Fletcher had regained consciousness; and whilst he was still weak, Doctor Wheston expected him to make a full recovery. Samuel elected to spend the evening keeping Johnny company at the magistrate's home whilst the others attended the ball. Mrs. Fletcher stayed home with the boys, but Mr. Fletcher put in an appearance for half an hour.

Elizabeth hardly recognised Bedlington Hall. For many years it had been a dark, sterile place, kept clean by the servants, but showing little signs of habitation beyond Lady Bedlington's boudoir and occasionally the dining room. The halls had been decked with sparkling Christmas decorations, and warm fires burned in every grate, whilst hundreds of candles illuminated the dark corners of every room.

Minstrels played in a gallery above the ballroom, and the dancing had already begun when Elizabeth arrived, escorted by Liam. Her father escorted the sisters, who though dressed in the same black lace, had attempted to brighten up their appearance with sprigs of holly, replete with red berries, attached to their shoulders. The effect was of two rather prickly shrubs. Doctor Wheston and Mrs. Wheston, who looked very pretty in a pale blue silk gown, arrived soon after.

Liam helped Elizabeth out of her cloak to reveal she wore a white off-the-shoulder gown of silk, with a large red sash around the centre. Her hair was pinned up with red ribbons. The dress was her mother's, as many of Elizabeth's clothes were, and her expert hands had brought the fashion up-to-date.

'You look very beautiful,' said Liam. He wore a long black jacket with a grey waistcoat over a crisp white shirt, with a white cravat and dark grey trousers.

'Thank you,' said Elizabeth, telling herself that it was the heat from all the candles making her cheeks feel so warm.

'What a spectacle!' said Mrs. Chatterbucks. The three men had gone to fetch drinks for the ladies.

'It is most exciting,' said Miss Graves. 'It is a long time since I have been to a ball.'

'I hope you will also enjoy yourself, Mrs. Wheston,' said Elizabeth.

'I am sure I shall.' Amelia Wheston smiled. Not for the first time, Elizabeth thought the lady very pretty. She could not blame Liam if he was in love with her, but following Amelia's eyes, it became clear to Elizabeth that she loved no man but her husband. She took in the information with immense relief. Yes, there was a definite affection between Mrs. Wheston and Liam, but it was of a purely platonic nature.

'Mr. Doubleday tells me that he brought good news of your brother,'

129

said Elizabeth. 'I hope he is well and that we may meet him one day.'

Amelia Wheston turned to Elizabeth and looked at her for what seemed a long time. 'I am sure you will,' said Amelia eventually. 'When you do, remember that Liam does enjoy his little jokes.'

'I'm sorry?'

'Never mind.' Amelia smiled kindly. 'Liam tells me that you have received an offer of marriage.'

'Really?' said Mrs. Chatterbucks.

'Well, I never,' said Miss Graves.

Elizabeth looked from one to the other, and was only saved from answering by the return of the men.

'I hope I did not speak out of turn,' said Amelia quietly, when they all had their drinks.

'Not at all,' said Elizabeth. 'No more than I did about your brother, I am sure.' Elizabeth felt certain that Amelia had brought up the subject of marriage to prevent any further conversation about her brother. She only had a moment to wonder why, because the festivities began soon after.

After ten minutes, and with all the guests assembled in the Great Hall, Lady Bedlington's arrival was announced. The whole room gasped when they saw that she descended the stairs accompanied by her step-daughter, Lady Clarissa. Lady Bedlington, as before, was dressed in black lace, befitting her age and station. But it was Lady Clarissa who caught everyone's attention. She wore a gown of the deepest, darkest red velvet, with a black sash, and a red velvet ribbon in her hair.

Elizabeth found herself looking at Liam, to gauge his reaction. How could he fail to be enchanted? But it was clear from his face, and from Lady Clarissa's as she passed them by with her step-mother, that they had never set eyes on each other until that moment.

'She is very lovely, is she not?' said Elizabeth, when the two ladies had passed by.

'She is certainly that,' said Liam. 'But sad, I think.'

'She has known sadness.'

'Yes, she was in love with the younger Sanderson brother, was she not?' Liam turned to her, and it was as if Lady Clarissa and her concerns had immediately been forgotten. 'Will you dance, Elizabeth?'

Elizabeth agreed, and lost herself in the music for the next twenty minutes as they joined in with the dancing. It was as if the recent murder had been forgotten, as everyone threw themselves into the Christmas spirit. Elizabeth had seldom known such joy in her aunt's house, which was usually austere. It was helped, she suspected, by the new-found closeness between Lady Bedlington and Lady Clarissa. She was curious to know what had happened to bring about such a rapprochement. Then she felt Liam's strong hand grip her waist and all other thoughts dissipated in the pleasure of his touch.

It was on the second, slower measure that she noticed the man in the minstrels' gallery. He was not one of the band, of that she was sure, and neither did he seem to be a guest. He merely sat there watching the dancing, with his eyes moving amongst the crowds of people, from the dancers to those taking a rest, then back again. He wore a new suit, and was clean enough, but he gave the impression that he was not used to wearing such fine clothes. He kept pulling at the collar of his shirt and tugging at the sleeves, as if the clothes on his back imprisoned him.

'I wonder . . . ' said Elizabeth, as Liam held her in his arms, 'who that strange man is.'

'I have no idea,' said Liam. 'I noticed him a short while ago. Perhaps he came with the band.'

'He is not playing an instrument.'

'No, but he may well help the band to carry theirs. I hear there are such men employed by the more successful musical troupes.'

'Oh yes, I should have thought of that.' But the answer did not satisfy her. The man was too interested in his surroundings. That might be the case had he never visited a grand house before, but it did not strike Elizabeth that the surroundings were particularly new to the man. If that were so, he would be taking in the furnishings and the architecture. What was more, she began to notice that his eyes often hesitated over Lady Clarissa, softening for a moment, before becoming hard again and resuming what appeared to be some sort of search.

At one point, Lady Clarissa looked up to the man, and he shook his head almost imperceptibly. Elizabeth looked around at the other guests. Only then did it strike her exactly how odd it was that her aunt, who had been a virtual recluse, should suddenly invite the whole town to a ball. And it was the whole town. Apart from Mr. and Miss Hardacre.

'I wonder where the Hardacres are,' said Elizabeth, whilst she and Liam took a rest from dancing and sipped eggnog.

'Are you wishing for more exciting company, Elizabeth?' asked Liam.

'Oh no, not at all. I'm having a wonderful time with you.' Elizabeth clamped her mouth shut. What was it about this man that made her speak so openly? 'What I mean is . . . '

'I am quite happy with your first answer,' he said. 'Come, waltz with me.'

'Do you think that perhaps you should give some of the other young men a chance to dance with Miss Dearheart?' said Amelia Wheston.

'I think that's a dreadful idea,' said Liam, leading Elizabeth to the dance floor once more. 'You don't mind, do you? That I am monopolising your time?'

'I don't mind,' said Elizabeth, feeling heady and warm because of the punch and eggnog she had drunk. Supper had not been served yet, and she had been too excited to eat anything before leaving the house. At least that was what she told herself. She was sure it had nothing to do with Liam's strong arm around her waist, and the way he held her small gloved hand in his.

She also felt more light-hearted than she had been of late. Liam was definitely not Albert Sanderson, because he and Lady Clarissa were strangers. And it was also certain that Liam and Amelia Wheston were not in love either. Amelia had danced with John Wheston most of the night, only taking a break to dance with Elizabeth's father. Despite Amelia's teasing words, Liam had danced with each of the sisters, as had the reverend. It threw Mrs. Chatterbucks and Miss Graves into flurries of excitement to be chosen by such handsome men. The memory of this night, thought Elizabeth, would be something to keep them warm in the cold winter nights that followed, and she had no doubt they would be talking about it for many years after that.

But the night seemed to belong to her and Liam. The music felt as though it had been written especially for them, the dances designed for the movement of their bodies. For the first time in many months Elizabeth felt as though she was where she belonged. How could she ever have thought about leaving Midchester when so much happiness could be found within its boundaries?

'I'm glad we had this time together,' said Liam, as the tempo changed and the music became slower still.

'It sounds as though you're going away,' said Elizabeth.

'That may happen soon,' he said. 'If it is not too forward of me, could I speak to you alone for a moment?'

Elizabeth followed him out of the warm ballroom and to the cooler atmosphere of the study. Though a fire burned in the grate, it was not so overwhelmingly warm as it had been amongst the heat of over fifty bodies in the ballroom. She pressed her gloves to her cheeks, which were slightly damp with perspiration.

'Elizabeth . . . ' Liam had walked to the fireplace and stood with his back to her, gazing into its depths.

'What is it?'

'I . . . I don't want you to think I've

misled you in any way about my feelings. You are . . . ' he paused, as if the words wouldn't come. 'I never thought I would find a woman who was so gentle and kind, and without artifice. You are all those things, and more. You're beautiful, you're intelligent . . . '

'But . . . ' Elizabeth croaked, sensing the next word. He would tell her that he only thought of her as a sister. It would not be the first time. Apart from Mr. Hardacre, most of the men — not that there had been many — that Elizabeth had liked had told her the same thing.

Liam spun around. 'But nothing. I adore you. I have loved you since the first moment I saw you. Only . . . I'm not free to love you, and I hold you in too much esteem to offer you any other option.'

'What are you trying to say?' Had she got it so wrong? Was there a connection between Liam and Lady Clarissa? Something they had hidden from everyone else? But then Lady Bedlington would have to be involved, and Elizabeth doubted her aunt's ability at such dissimulation.

'I never meant to mislead you, I swear. My feelings overtook me and I am afraid I acted too rashly in speaking to you as I did. Elizabeth . . . remember that I told you I once had a wife and did not wish to repeat the experience?'

'Yes . . . '

'As far as I know, she is still living. I am still married.'

'No!' She put her hands to her face in horror.

'I wish it were different. I wish I could find my wife and divorce her, then I could be with . . . '

'No.' Elizabeth shook her head vehemently. 'No, I would not allow that. If your vows to her are so easy to break, how could I ever trust you to be constant?' Despite her feelings for him, it horrified her to think he would be quite happy to rid himself of his wife.

'Then I have disappointed you.'

'No . . . yes. You should not have let me think . . . ' Elizabeth felt tears stinging her eyes. Her head spun, trying to assimilate the new information. 'And everyone else. Oh, what will people think? I let you escort me to this ball. My father was deceived too.'

'You have no idea of the hell I've suffered, Lizzie, married to a woman who deceived me, who would have been happy to see me die.'

'If you are trying to come up with excuses for breaking your marriage vows, be clear that I will not accept any of them. Despite living in such a small town I am aware of the lies men tell about their wives. How she does not understand him. How she does not let him . . . does not honour his conjugal rights. Please do not do me the disservice of lying in such a way. It will only make me hate you, and . . . ' Her voice broke. 'On second thought, do say all that. It would be easier to hate you. Much easier than this pain I'm feeling now.' She gulped back a sob.

'My wife framed me for murder, Lizzie. Then she left me to rot in prison.'

'What? Then you are Albert Sanderson?

Oh dear God, then it is not only me you have deceived, but Lady Clarissa.' She realised on some level that it didn't ring true. Albert Sanderson had not gone to prison. Unless Liam were speaking figuratively. She imagined a sanatorium might feel much like a prison.

'I am not Albert Sanderson. Though it seems he and I have much in common.'

She sensed rather than heard the door to the study open wider.

'I want you to know that whatever people may tell you about me in the future, I am not the man they have made me out to be. And I am not an inconstant husband. At least no more than my wife is an inconstant wife.' Liam was looking over her shoulder at something.

Elizabeth turned her head, and was vaguely aware of Constable Hounds standing at the door. He was watching them. Elizabeth felt a dart of panic in her breast. 'What is it?'

The constable gave an apologetic

cough and came into the room. He had several other men with him, and behind him in the hall some of the guests had stopped to see what was going on. Elizabeth recognised the other men as local farm workers who were often deputised to help during trouble in the neighbourhood. As if on cue, the music in the ballroom stopped and everyone stood still, awaiting the next move.

Constable Hounds reached and spoke to Liam. 'Doctor William Bradbourne, I am arresting you for murder and your subsequent escape from jail. Now, be a good man and come quietly.'

Elizabeth looked up at Liam, expecting him to say it was preposterous, but he merely nodded.

'Liam!' Amelia shot through the crowds. 'Liam, darling!'

'Take care of her, John,' Liam said to Doctor Wheston, who had followed his wife.

'Dearest, tell them,' said Amelia, grabbing Liam by the sleeve. 'Tell them that she's still alive somewhere and that she's the one who murdered your patient. Constable Hounds, you must believe me when I say my brother is guilty of nothing. He is a good man!'

That was when it all became clear to Elizabeth. Of course Liam had brought good news of Amelia's brother. He had brought himself.

'I'm sorry, Mrs. Wheston,' said Constable Hounds. 'I have to do my job, as painful as it is. I . . . I like Doctor Doubleday — Doctor Bradbourne. But he has been found guilty of murder and I must do my duty.'

If Elizabeth's head spun at the news of Liam being married, it was nothing compared to how it whirled with the news that he was a condemned man. But he had touched her, and looked at her with love in his eyes. He had saved her brother's and Johnny Fletcher's lives. Had he really been the murderer they were seeking, it would have been better to leave them both to die in the icy pond. She shivered at the thought of losing Samuel that way. But nothing she had known about Liam in the past few days pointed to him being capable of taking a life.

Of course she could be deluding herself, because she knew that whatever else might be a lie, her feelings for him were not. She was hopelessly in love with him. Perhaps it blinded her to his faults, but everything else in her body cried out that he was being unjustly treated.

'I'm sorry, Elizabeth,' said Liam, taking her hand in his and kissing it. 'For one solitary moment I had a dream of a quiet life with a woman I truly loved, but I would have been pretending for all of it. This is why I wanted to be honest with you. You are a beacon of hope and truth in a dark world, and I was drawn to your purity. But I won't involve you in my darkness. Forget all I said. Pretend it was all a wonderful dream that you and I once shared. If it helps you to believe I am a murderer, then so be it, because I would rather you hated me than go to my death knowing that I caused you a moment's pain.'

His words were like a knife to her heart. How could she feel anything but pain when she thought of him, dangling from the end of a hangman's noose, his handsome face contorted in agony?

'I'm sorry, Doctor Bradbourne, but we must go . . . ' said Constable Hounds. They started towards the door and went out into the hall.

Elizabeth thought she might collapse with grief, only to feel her father's steadying arm on her shoulder. 'Father . . . ' she whispered, through her tears. She put her head on the reverend's shoulder. She was aware of all eyes on her, judging her.

'Shh, my child.'

'Father,' she said quietly, 'I am sorry if I have brought shame on you, but I love him.'

'I could never be ashamed of you, Lizzie.'

'Everyone else will think . . . ' But what did it matter? Liam was being taken away, where no doubt he would be executed. The thought was like a thousand knives stabbing her.

'Let them think what they will,' said Reverend Dearheart. 'Love does not always send us the people that society thinks are right for us, but let society worry about its own affairs. We will do what we can for Liam, to make his last days as peaceful as possible.'

'Oh no . . . ' At that, Elizabeth lost all control and sobbed into her father's shoulder.

As the constable and his men left with Liam, slamming the front door behind them, Elizabeth instinctively looked up into the minstrels' gallery. The man who had been sitting there had disappeared.

8

The assembled townspeople burst into a rhapsody of gossip as soon as the constable and his men took Liam away.

Lady Clarissa, ignoring some stern words from her step-mother, crossed the room to Elizabeth and Amelia Wheston. 'Be of good cheer,' she said. 'Help is at hand.'

'What help could there be?' asked Amelia. Her husband still held her in his arms. 'Liam is doomed.'

'I cannot say yet as it would put someone I . . . someone who is important to me in danger. But we will help to free your brother, that I promise, Mrs. Wheston.' Although she addressed Amelia Wheston, Lady Clarissa's eyes fell upon Elizabeth with a depth of understanding that made Elizabeth feel that they were kindred spirits. 'I know what it is to love a condemned man. Please, rest tonight and be assured that you have friends.' With that, Lady Clarissa climbed the staircase to the upper level and disappeared into the shadows.

'Come,' said the reverend. 'Whilst Lady Clarissa's offer of help has strong foundations, we will repair to the vicarage and find out what we can do for those we love.'

'He will need a good lawyer,' said Amelia. She turned to Elizabeth. 'You must believe that he is the kindest, gentlest of men. He is not a killer.'

'But he's the Demon Doctor of Delhi,' said Mrs. Chatterbucks, who had dashed across the room several minutes earlier to hear what the constable had to say.

'He is not a demon!' Amelia's eyes blazed. 'Oh I hate journalists, and all the dreadful things they make up about people.' She burst into tears, and was once again comforted by her husband.

'My wife speaks the truth,' said Doctor Wheston. 'I taught Liam in medical school. He is no monster. He has dedicated his career to saving lives, not taking them.'

The sisters had the grace to look chastened. 'I am sure he seems like a very good man,' said Miss Graves. 'In fact I was only saying to my dear sister yesterday that it was pleasant to have such a handsome young man in the district.'

'Certainly,' said Mrs. Chatterbucks. Elizabeth understood that Amelia's tears showed them a different side to the sensational stories they read in the papers. Here was real human suffering, from the family of a man unjustly condemned.

★   ★   ★

It was very early on Christmas Day morning when Elizabeth visited Liam at the gaol. She had barely slept. She, her father and the Whestons had talked late into the night about what steps could be taken to help him.

All Elizabeth's misgivings about his marital status had, for the moment, disappeared. All she cared about was saving his life. What happened afterwards was left to fate. Taking a plate of warm bacon and bread and a mug of coffee to the gaol, she told herself that it was only Christian charity, when in her heart she knew that she could not leave him alone on Christmas morning, feeling that he had no friends. Not that Amelia and John Wheston didn't show the same concern, but by the time they said goodnight, Amelia was clearly exhausted by her emotions. Elizabeth realised that she had only been dealing with the horror of Liam's predicament for one night and that was bad enough. Amelia must have spent months in abject despair at the thought of her brother's imminent execution, and then suffered even more stress when he escaped, not knowing if he had made it to safety until he arrived in Midchester. No wonder she had run out to embrace him on the night they returned from Lady Bedlington's. Even though she had seen him when he arrived, she must have felt a sense of relief every time Liam returned safely to her house over the following days.

The gaol was a small hut-like building attached to the constable's cottage. Luckily for Elizabeth, Constable Hounds and his wife were already awake. 'I've brought Doctor Doubleday . . . I mean Doctor Bradbourne, some food,' she explained.

'Oh, there was no need, Miss Dearheart,' said the constable's wife, Kitty. 'I've made bread for him, and coffee. But I'll not say he won't be glad of some bacon too. He's a nice young man.'

'He's a convicted murderer,' said Constable Hounds. But there was something in his voice. Some element of doubt. 'Not that he seems like one. Very gentleman-like, he is. But it could be an act, so mind yourself, Miss Dearheart.'

'May I see him?' asked Elizabeth. 'My father will be along after the morning service.'

'For a few minutes. They're coming

to fetch him later on this morning, to take him to a bigger gaol. Where . . . ' As if realising he was touching on painful territory, the constable clamped his mouth shut. He led her through the back room, to a small door which led into the gaol. It was of solid wood, with bars at the top. The constable unlocked the door and murmured, 'I'll be standing by in case of trouble.' He took a position outside the door, leaving it slightly ajar.

'Elizabeth . . . ' Liam's voice was full of despair when he saw her. 'You shouldn't have come here, my love.' He had been sitting on the truckle bed, but stood up when he saw her. In this tiny room he looked even larger than ever. His deep-set eyes were lined with dark circles.

'I had to see you,' she whispered. 'I need to know the truth. Did you kill him?'

'No!' Liam sat back down and put his head in his hands. 'I am not a killer, Elizabeth, I swear it.' Elizabeth put the food down on the floor and sat on a rickety chair next to the bed. 'I have no need to take my patients' money. Our family are rich in our own right. Only, my wife had other ideas.'

'Tell me what happened, Liam.'

He looked up at her. 'It took this for you to call me by my first name?'

Elizabeth blushed. 'It is one way of breaking the ice, I suppose. Did you love her very much?' It was strange how the answer to that question was more important to her than the tragic death of an innocent man. She was a humane enough girl to feel shame at her own selfishness.

'I thought I did at first. Clara brought out the protective instincts in me. She arrived in Delhi just over a year ago, a frail, helpless creature. She told me, and others, that she had fled her brother, who controlled her whole life, and was often abusive to her. Then one night she arrived at my house with a bruise on her cheek. She said that her brother had found her and that he was trying to force her into marriage with an elderly man. So I offered to marry her, to save her from it. At least, I thought I had offered at the time. Now, when I look back on it, I can see that she led me to that conclusion. She had said something like, 'Of course, if we were already married'. Don't you see how it was? She was a woman in trouble, and I felt I had to help her escape her cruel brother.'

'Yes, I understand,' said Elizabeth. She could almost see the scene as Liam described it — the stricken woman and the kind man whose very vocation led him to protect and nurture.

'It was not a marriage in the true sense of the word.' Liam seemed to hesitate. 'What I mean is that I did not insist on the rights of a husband, and she seemed relieved that I left her in peace. I had not saved her from one awful marriage to inflict anything upon her that would make her unhappy.' He paused. 'And I don't say this to deceive you. There have been women in my life. Discreet affairs. I am no saint.'

'I understand,' said Elizabeth. For some reason it made her feel happy to know he had not made love to his wife, even though there was no moral reason why he should not, and probably a dozen moral reasons why he should not have had lovers before his marriage, if one followed the teachings of the Bible. But Elizabeth's own sexual awakening, and the longing she felt for him, had taught her that what one should do, and what the body told one to do, were quite different things. Plus, it was implausible that a man of Liam's age and latent sensuality could have spent his adult life as a celibate.

'Then a colleague approached me one day, another doctor. He warned me away from Clara. She had visited his wife, and told her that I had behaved in an abusive manner towards her. She apparently showed this good woman a bruise on her arm, which she said I inflicted upon her. You can only imagine what they thought of me. I swear, Elizabeth, I have never struck a woman in my life.

I would never behave that way.'

'I believe you. Did you ask her about it? Clara, I mean.'

'Yes, I confronted her that evening at dinner. I tried to make it seem that the lady had misunderstood her, so as not to apportion blame. She left the room in tears, refusing to discuss it. That was the last time I saw her. The following morning she had gone, along with all her clothes, and at the same time my patient was found dead. Then the police in Delhi received an anonymous note saying that I had murdered the patient. He had died of an overdose of morphine. It was from an ampoule I had signed for at a local apothecary. They found a scrap of paper in my study that they say proved I had been practising how to forge his signature. Then the other doctor's wife came forward with what she knew, about my supposed brutality, which added to the hysteria surrounding it all. It was only then I found that Clara had been telling everyone that I mistreated her. The evidence, as far as the police were concerned, was overwhelming. I was not only a murderer, but a wife-beater too. I was tried and convicted. But by that time the friend who had first come to me with his concerns had second thoughts about it all, despite his wife's hysteria. So he helped me to escape. I came here, to look for my sister. To let her know I was safe.' He took a deep breath. 'This has been dreadful for her, and for John. She has maintained my innocence all along. She knows me, and she knows I am not a killer.'

'How old was Clara?' asked Elizabeth.

'She was thirty-two when we met.' Liam frowned. 'What has that got to do with anything?'

Elizabeth told him about the two Lucindas: Lucinda Hargreaves, who had disappeared after murdering her husband, and the Lucinda who had married Albert Sanderson. 'I am just trying to ascertain whether there was one Lucinda or two. And also whether your wife Clara is the same person as Prudence Rivers. I think it's a plot, you see.' Elizabeth took a deep breath and tried to order her own thoughts before explaining her suspicions to Liam. 'The first Lucinda Hargreaves was the mother of two children who fled Midchester. She murdered her husband. When it was too late, she might have realized there were other ways. What if either she, or a different Lucinda — her daughter perhaps — decided that rather than bring suspicion upon herself, she would frame someone else for it? Then once the husband had been executed, all she had to do was return and claim his fortune. So she would benefit twice from the crime: once from embezzling the money off the first victim, and then from the executed husband. She probably hoped the same would happen to Albert Sanderson, but he was mentally ill, so could not be sent for trial. Are you ... are you very rich, Liam?'

'Our family owns many properties in Ireland. Not to mention what I've earned as a doctor. It has left both Amelia and myself with a more than generous annuity. The problem with an annuity, Elizabeth, is that it would rely on the bank and solicitors knowing where the person who inherited lives. I can't see that your Lucinda or Prudence or Clara would risk that. It would be something to tie her to each executed husband.'

'Unless . . . ' said Elizabeth, thinking hard. 'Unless she was able to persuade the family who should have inherited that she would go away and forget about it. In return for a lump sum.'

'That's what happened in the Rivers case,' said Constable Hounds, causing both Elizabeth and Liam to jump. They had forgotten he was there. 'A friend from their village told me about it. The young lady agreed to a cash sum of two hundred pounds to go away and make no further claims on the estate. I gather the Rivers family had to sell some stock in order to make up the amount, but it meant the annuity went to Bertram Rivers' nephew, which was the original intention.'

'Constable Hounds, please help us,' said Elizabeth, standing up. 'You know this is an injustice, don't you? Couldn't you let Doctor Bradbourne go for now, so we can look into this together?'

'I can see there's questions that need to be asked, Miss Dearheart, yes. But I can't let this young man go. Not until they're answered. He's still an escaped convict.'

'But surely if there has been an injustice, then he should never have been in prison.'

'The law is the law, Miss Dearheart, you know that.'

'Then I will find out the truth,' said Elizabeth. She turned to Liam. 'I never thought of it before, but I'll go and look in the parish records. They may mention Lucinda Hargreaves and her two children.'

Liam stood up and took her hands in his. 'You're wonderful,' he said. And completely oblivious to the constable's presence and his own marital status, he took Elizabeth into his arms and kissed her. For the first time she knew what a kiss should be, as she gave herself up entirely to the love she felt for him. He pulled away reluctantly. 'Whatever happens, I will never forget what you're trying to do for me, Elizabeth. I'll take the memory of it to my grave.'

'Shh,' said Elizabeth, putting her fingers to his lips. Her eyes filled with tears, and for one horrible moment she saw the shadow of the hangman's noose over Liam's head. Any moral qualms she'd had the night before had disappeared. Yes, he was married, but to a woman who would have happily seen him executed. Surely God would forgive her the sin of loving him. 'Please don't think like that. We . . . I will . . . clear your name, Liam. I promise.'

Elizabeth left Liam in Constable and Mrs. Hounds' capable hands. 'It does the heart good to see two young people in love,' said Kitty Hounds, wiping her eyes on her apron. 'You take care, Miss Dearheart. Don't you go getting into any danger.'

With a promise that she would keep safe, Elizabeth made her way to the church. She could hear the choir singing carols as she grew nearer, and she was reminded once again that it was Christmas morning. Samuel would be waking soon, eager for his presents, and for the first time since he had been born she was not there to see the new day in with him. It made her think about what would happen if she went away. Seeing her brother's face on Christmas morning had been amongst the joys of her life.

Pushing the thought aside for the moment, she went around the back of the church and in through the vestry door. The singing was louder in there, and through a crack in the door leading to the altar she could see several villagers already seated in the pews praying, including Mrs. Chatterbucks and Miss Graves. They had their eyes closed in reverent prayer, though Elizabeth could not help noticing with a smile that every now and then one of them opened their eyes as if to check everyone else was being just as reverent.

She slipped past them, praying not to be seen. Her father also had his head bowed in prayer, but she had no doubt he would sense her presence. He looked up slightly with a questioning look in his eyes. She put her fingers to her lips, and went to the vestry.

Elizabeth opened the various cupboards in the vestry and searched through the records of births, deaths and marriages. She tried to remember whether it had been said that Lucinda Hargreaves's children had been born in Midchester, or whether she had arrived with them. If she had arrived with them, then there would be no record of their birth. So she contented herself with finding the marriage record, in the hopes that might throw some light on the subject. She found the record, but all it told her was that Lucinda Yates had married Franklin Hargreaves thirty-three years previously. Elizabeth checked the record of deaths, and sure enough

Franklin Hargreaves was listed as deceased, some three years after the marriage.

Next Elizabeth took out the record of baptisms at the church. She had little hope of finding anything, and decided to work back from the date of Lucinda and Franklin's marriage, for no other reason than that it was the one date of which she could be certain. She did not have to look for long. For on the same day that Lucinda and Franklin married, it was recorded that two children, a boy aged three and a girl aged two, were baptised. She had no time to wonder at the events that led to the parents marrying some time after the children were born. She had known of people in the village who had not bothered to marry, but it was felt amongst the townspeople that they were not quite nice to know. However, her father always treated them kindly, in the hopes that one day they would feel encouraged to marry under God's holy laws. Elizabeth ran her hands over the Christian names of the two children, and realised then that she had the whole story at her fingertips.

It had been such an easy deception, she mused, as she carried the book out of the church, and out to the street. All it took was to change part of the surname, and an occasional change of Christian names, and no one would ever suspect. Then when the mother became too old to attract men, or died, the daughter took over. Possibly the son too. Elizabeth had not forgotten about the case in France mentioned in the newspaper. She thought about her own annuity of one hundred pounds a year, but also what she might inherit from Lady Bedlington, who could not live for many more years. It made her a very attractive prospect to the wrong man. And she had known he was the wrong man the moment he proposed to her. It was not only her burgeoning feelings for Liam that had prevented her from feeling attraction. It was the strong sense that something was not quite right.

9

When Elizabeth reached the gaol, it was to find a commotion. Over at the gaol, two officers stood either side of Liam, who, it broke her heart to see, had been put in manacles. There was a carriage outside the constable's gate. It was closed in, with only a small, barred window at the back, and the sight of it chilled her far more than the cold winter air. They had come to take him, but were prevented from moving by an obstruction.

There was another carriage in the centre of the road, overloaded with trunks and household belongings. One of the horses had gone lame. Mr. Hardacre stood beside the horse, beating it furiously with a stick, whilst it cowed its head in supplication. Elizabeth gasped in horror on seeing the vicious look on Hardacre's face and the suffering of the poor animal.

'Come now, Mr. Hardacre,' said Constable Hounds. 'Don't treat the animal so. We'll get the smithy out, and find you a new horse.'

'Get up, you beast!' yelled Hardacre. 'Move, damn it, or I'll kill you!'

'Well, I never,' said Mrs. Chatterbucks, who had left the church some time earlier with her sister to return home for breakfast. They stood at the side of the roadway, watching the horror unfold. 'Such language. Such behavior, and from a gentleman too.'

'He's no gentleman,' said Elizabeth. She crossed the road to where Hardacre stood. 'Cedric Hargreaves,' she cried, 'you stop that this instant!'

Her use of his real name had the desired effect. Hardacre stopped, his eyes wild with anger. His manner changed within seconds, and for the first time, Elizabeth saw the real danger in the man. A man who could switch from brutality to charm in a matter of seconds. How might such a man treat a wife? 'I . . . I am sorry, Miss Dearheart.

You must forgive me. My sister and I are leaving Midchester. We're off to a warmer climate for her health. It is only my desire to ensure she is well that has led to this . . . this aberration, I assure you.' From the look in his eyes, he was clearly puzzled about the way she had addressed him.

'Where is your sister?' asked Elizabeth. 'Is she in the carriage?' Elizabeth walked to the carriage door.

'Stop!' said Hardacre. 'She is wrapped up warm, and I am sure you do not wish to add to her sickness by letting the cold in.'

'Why? Are you afraid that Doctor Bradbourne might recognise his wife?'

Hardacre became flustered. 'I am not sure what you mean.'

'Constable Hounds,' Elizabeth called across the street, 'please have your men bring Doctor Bradbourne here.'

The constable did as Elizabeth asked. The men crossed the street with Liam and brought him around to where Elizabeth stood.

'Oh, I see where this is going,' said Cedric Hardacre. 'You will say she is your wife just to clear your name. Never mind that you've never set eyes on my sister before.'

Ignoring him, Elizabeth yanked the door open to reveal Dora Hardacre, sitting in the carriage, shaking with fear. Elizabeth could see that it was not the fear of being harmed. It was the fear of being found out. 'I've never seen this man before in my life,' said Dora, before Liam could speak.

'That's odd,' said Liam. 'Because I certainly know you, Clara. As will the people you met in Delhi. So I suggest you and your brother stay in Midchester, until they can get here.'

'We will do no such thing,' said Cedric Hardacre. 'This is nothing to do with us.'

'You were born to Lucinda Yates,' said Elizabeth. 'Probably out of wedlock. Thirty-three years ago, she married Franklin Hargreaves. I imagine she'd already set up her plan to have him framed for murder. You and your brother were baptised on the day of their wedding. I have it here.' Elizabeth held out the book. 'Cedric and Dora Hargreaves. You returned recently, in the hopes that no one would recognise you. And you were correct. No one did. Until Mr. Sanderson visited on business. My guess is that he saw your sister in the village and recognised her as the young woman who had married his brother, Albert. You,' she turned to Mr. Hardacre, 'agreed to meet him, and killed him. Then as if that were not bad enough, you insulted his memory by turning him into a snowman.'

'This is preposterous,' said Dora. 'I am not that woman.'

'Yes you are,' said a voice from the assembled crowd. A man stepped forward, and next to him a hooded lady. It was the man whom Elizabeth had seen sitting in the minstrels' gallery. The woman removed the hood and revealed herself to be Lady Clarissa. 'I am Albert Sanderson, and this woman is my wife, Lucinda.' He pointed to Dora.

'I persuaded my step-mother to hold a Christmas ball,' said Lady Clarissa.

'We invited everyone in the district. Albert . . . ' She looked at Sanderson, and Elizabeth saw the sadness in Clarissa's eyes disappear to be replaced by enduring love. They became harder when she looked again upon Cedric and Dora Hardacre. 'Albert sat in the minstrels' gallery, in the hopes he would see you amongst the crowd, Lucinda. When that did not work, we started looking at who had not taken up the invitation. The Hardacre brother and sister were the only ones. You can imagine our interest when we heard you were thinking of leaving soon. We've had people watching you, and as soon as we heard you had packed up early, we came down here to stop you. Luckily the horse did that for us. Poor creature.' Clarissa's eyes softened as she looked at the horse, but she could easily have been talking about the tired and sad man who stood next to her.

'So it was not Mr. Sanderson who told the constable about Liam?' said Elizabeth.

'No,' said Lady Clarissa, smiling. 'I imagine Mr. Hardacre did that when his sister saw Doctor Bradbourne from a distance the other day.'

'But they waited until last night so that the commotion surrounding his arrest would cover their departure,' said Elizabeth, catching on quickly. She remembered how confused and upset Liam had been when she was on her way to visit the Hardacres. At the time she assumed he had seen Lady Clarissa. It must have been Dora Hardacre, the woman he knew as Clara.

'You are a very intelligent young woman, Miss Dearheart,' said Lady Clarissa.

'Was it you who chased my brother and Johnny Fletcher?' asked Elizabeth, advancing on Cedric Hardacre. 'Because I do not believe for one minute it was Mr. Sanderson, although I'm sure it was your intention to have us believe that.'

'I'm telling you, this is preposterous,' said Hardacre.

'Your sister has been recognised by

two men. Shall we contact the Rivers family and see if they recognise her as Prudence Rivers? And what about the lady in France? Would her family recognise you as the husband who turned up after that tragic lady had been executed?'

'He made me do it,' said Dora Hardacre, whining. 'Do you not see how it is, Liam, darling? How he made me deceive you? And you, Albert. I knew you loved Lady Clarissa. I said to him, 'Please don't make me do this to such a good man.' But he has beaten and cajoled me all our lives.'

'You lying wretch!' Hardacre cried. 'It was your idea to carry on Mother's schemes. It would make us rich, you said. And we have scraped all our lives. Miss Dearheart, I only asked you to marry me so I could escape her forever.'

The brother and sister bickered on that theme, whilst the constables unlocked Liam's manacles and transferred them to Hardacre. They fetched more manacles for Dora, and both were put into the black van originally intended for Liam and carried away. They could be heard screaming and shouting at each other as the van disappeared down the street.

10

The list of guests for Christmas luncheon had swelled so much that Lady Bedlington insisted on hosting it at Bedlington Hall. Elizabeth, Samuel and the Reverend Dearheart attended, along with Lady Clarissa and Albert Sanderson, the constable and his wife, Mrs. Chatterbucks and Miss Graves, John and Amelia Wheston, the Fletchers — with Johnny, who had awoken during the night and seemed to be on good form, though still pale — and Liam.

They began with a prayer for all those who had suffered at the hands of Cedric and Dora Hargreaves/Hardacre, especially the tragic victims either murdered or executed for crimes they had not committed.

'I am an old woman,' said Lady Bedlington as the soup was served, 'and I daresay I don't always take notice of what goes on around me, but could someone please explain to me how Mr. Sanderson here and Doctor Double-day . . . '

'Bradbourne,' Liam corrected her.

'Bradbourne . . . could both be married to the same woman? It is bigamy, and quite outrageous.'

'It means,' said Liam with a smile, 'that my marriage to Dora . . . or Clara, as I knew her . . . was not legal. I aim to see a lawyer to ensure that is the case, of course, but an annulment will be imminent so that I am finally free to marry again.' He looked at Elizabeth as he spoke. For her part, with all eyes upon her, she found her minestrone soup suddenly very interesting.

'I, too, will be seeking an annulment,' said Albert Sanderson. 'Our marriage was never consummated.'

'Really!' Lady Bedlington dropped her spoon. 'I don't think this is a proper discussion to be having at the luncheon table.'

'Lucinda . . . Dora's reason,' said

176

Albert Sanderson, carrying on regardless, 'was that her mother had despised children, and she was not going to make the same mistake.'

'I think,' said Elizabeth, 'that much might have been true. It was perhaps not so bad when the children were little. Their mother could use them as leverage. The poor, unfortunate widow left with two young children. As they grew older, then their age would have given her age away, reminding her, and others, that she was no longer a young woman capable of attracting a well-to-do husband. I would feel sorry for them — Mr. and Miss Hardacre — born into such a life, if not for the pain they have inflicted on others since.'

'So they were marrying people, embezzling money from their spouses' colleagues, then having the spouse arrested for murder?' said Mrs. Chatterbucks.

'Yes, that is correct,' said Elizabeth. 'In that way they gained twice: once from the embezzlement, then from the death of the spouse. It makes my blood run cold to think . . . ' She looked across at Liam. He had come so close to being taken away from her forever.

'What happened to their mother?' asked Miss Graves.

'Well,' said Elizabeth, choosing her words carefully, her lips curling slightly, 'at one point I suspected that you were the real Lucinda Hargreaves.'

Miss Graves blushed, flustered, but then seemed to suppress a smile. 'Me, a cold-blooded femme fatale. Why, the very thought!'

'Of course,' said Mrs. Chatterbucks, not to be outdone, 'it would take a woman who had been married to know how to attract a man. You have never been married, dear.'

'Are you confessing to the crime, Mrs. Chatterbucks?' said Liam, with a smile.

'I most certainly am not! Though I daresay that in my younger days, I might have had the feminine wiles to pull such a crime off.'

'The mother is dead,' said Constable Hounds, after everyone had stopped laughing. 'They said so on the way to the gaol. She died in France.'

'It was strange,' said Albert Sanderson, 'but I never met her brother. He was always some shadowy ogre she mentioned.'

'The same here,' said Liam.

'I imagine,' said Elizabeth, 'it was better for them not to be seen together.'

'They were here, in Midchester,' said Mrs. Chatterbucks.

'Yes, but I don't think they came here to con anyone into marriage,' said Elizabeth. 'At least not at first. They came here to hide until Liam . . . Doctor Bradbourne . . . was executed. Dora only went into hiding properly when Mr. Sanderson's brother saw her. I think Mr. Hardacre's proposal to me was a last-ditch attempt to get their hands on some money whilst they waited for that event. I'm afraid that Aunt Arabella might then have been in desperate danger.'

Judging by Lady Bedlington's bright

eyes, that idea thrilled her almost as much as the sisters being femme fatales had excited them.

'It was something of a coincidence, your sister coming here, Doctor Bradbourne,' said Miss Graves.

'Not exactly,' said Amelia Wheston. 'You see, Liam had written a letter in which he said his wife, Clara — as he knew her — had mentioned Midchester as somewhere she had family, and that her mother's name had been Lucinda. So my husband and I came here to see if we could find the family. Of course, not having been to India, I had never met her, and did not know her real name.'

'All these names,' said Lady Bedlington. 'Dora, Clara, Lucinda, Prudence. I cannot keep up with it.'

'I rather think that was the idea,' said Elizabeth. 'No one would connect the names.'

'I suppose you are going to marry Mr. Sanderson now, Clarissa?' asked Lady Bedlington.

'I will as soon as his annulment comes through,' said Lady Clarissa. 'If that is . . . ' She looked at Albert Sanderson.

'If I want to?' he said. His face, ravaged by time and illness, became suddenly young again. 'It is all I have wanted for the past fifteen years. I can think of nothing that would make me happier.'

'So was it Hardacre who chased my Johnny and your Samuel?' said Mrs. Fletcher, speaking for the first time. 'Or was it Mr. Sanderson?'

'It was Hardacre,' said Albert Sanderson. 'Though I should confess that Johnny did see me near to the . . . my brother on the day Miss Dearheart found him. But I did not kill him. I went looking for him, having heard at the inn that he had gone there to meet someone. I cannot describe to you the treatments I have been given over the years. Certainly not in this mixed company. I can only tell you that they have sometimes left me with a feeling of unreality. Of not knowing what I truly saw and what I imagined in my head. When I saw my brother covered in snow, I convinced myself it was one of those moments when I saw things that were not there. I was terrified, but only as if in a nightmare. I did not know that what I saw was real. If I had realised . . . he might still be alive.'

Lady Clarissa reached out her hand for him. 'Hush now, my love. You must not punish yourself for the things others have done.'

After luncheon, there were the usual parlour games and singing at the piano, but it became clear that it was all too much for Albert Sanderson. He took himself off somewhere quiet, accompanied by Lady Clarissa. Liam stood at the fireplace with Elizabeth. 'The poor man,' he said. 'Some of the treatments for mental illness are barbaric. I only hope that with her love and kindness he will recover.'

'Yes, so do I,' said Elizabeth. 'She has been very patient, hasn't she? Waiting all this time for him. It must be wonderful to love and be loved like that.'

'Will you come for a walk with me, Elizabeth? I should like to speak to you alone.'

Elizabeth nodded and went to fetch her cloak. There was something in his voice that she feared was goodbye. She made up her mind to let him go. They had been brought together in dramatic circumstances, so she would not hold him to any promises he had made, or the kiss he had given her. He was a free man, or would be as soon as his marriage was properly declared null and void. She was suddenly shamed again by the idea that he had kissed her as a married man, for even if he had suspected his wife was alive, he did not know that the woman he knew as Clara was already married to another. What was more, Elizabeth had permitted it. What must he think of her behaviour? And why did it matter to her more now than when she had accepted the kiss?

Therefore, their walk together started awkwardly, with each lost in their own thoughts and feelings. The snow crackled under their feet, and turned Lady Bedlington's garden into a winter wonderland.

'I think the snow may be passing over,' said Elizabeth, falling back on that stalwart of English conversation, the weather. 'But spring still feels a long way off.'

'Yes, these dark days can make it seem so. But one morning you'll wake up and there will be daffodils in Midchester.'

'I imagine it's very hot in India. Even now.'

'Yes, it's very humid. They do have dust storms, and rains of course. They're not quite as pretty as snowfall.'

'Do you miss being there?'

'Yes and no. I have not had my happiest times in that city. I will have to return, of course.'

'Oh.'

'To clear everything up. Don't forget that I escaped from prison,' said Liam.

'They won't be happy about that even if I had been wrongly condemned.'

'But surely they won't censure you for that, given that you were innocent all along.'

'I should think not. But I also need to go there to ensure the annulment.'

'Yes, of course. Will you stay then? Once all is sorted out.' Elizabeth felt that her very life depended on the answer to the question.

'Actually, John is looking for a partner here in Midchester.'

'So you'll return?' Elizabeth tried to keep the excitement out of her voice.

'I may. It's just . . . '

'What?'

'I'm told that you wish to leave this place.'

'I did, for a while. But when I didn't see Samuel and my father at breakfast on Christmas morning, I realised what I would be losing by going. Not that I wouldn't like to travel one day. But I think I should always want to come home. I daresay that sounds very dull to you, who have travelled so much.'

'No, it sounds perfect.' He stopped walking and took her gloved hand. 'Elizabeth.'

She became shy, remembering his status as a married man, even if only technically so. 'I think perhaps we should behave circumspectly,' she said.

'Oh bother being circumspect. I love you, Elizabeth. I've loved you from the first moment I saw you, kneeling by that poor man in the snow. I had forgotten that a woman could be so kind and compassionate.' Liam pulled her into his arms. 'I know that I said that after having one wife I did not want another, but I was angry and bitter when I said that. I knew I had been duped, only with no idea to what extent. But now I know the truth, I also know that Dora or Clara or whatever her darned name is, is not typical of all women. She is certainly not you. I won't force my attentions on you, not with things as they are, but can I at least extract a promise from you that when my name is cleared, and I am a free man in every sense of the word, you will be waiting for me when I return to Midchester?'

'I promise.'

★   ★   ★

The months passed, with winter turning into spring. As Liam had promised, Elizabeth looked outside one morning and saw daffodils growing in the gardens and on the verges of the roads in the village. Midchester, after its long winter nap, was coming alive again, with fairs and markets, and the promise of a new day. The pond rippled with new life, and the spectre of George Sanderson encased in snow had disappeared with the cold. The only cloud was that Elizabeth had not heard from Liam for a week or more. She knew things had gone well in India, because he had written and told her. Under the circumstances, Liam was cleared of all wrongdoing, and the fact of his escape was understood as the act of an innocent and desperate man.

So it was with a heavy heart that she set out to the village square one morning to fetch provisions. She had been able to discard her winter coat, and wore a pretty dress with white and blue stripes. With a sigh, she entered the baker's and bought two loaves of bread. Then she went along to the grocery store for flour and eggs. She thought of making a cake for Samuel's tea. He had invited Johnny Fletcher over. But none of these preparations filled the ache in her heart.

Perhaps, she thought, her initial feelings were right. That she and Liam had come together under extreme circumstances. He had not promised her marriage. He had only asked that she would wait for him. So she had waited. In her heart, she still waited. Only her mind, annoyingly sensible to the end, told her that he had merely seen her as a sympathetic soul at a time when his life was at its lowest ebb. Now back in India, he would no doubt fall back into his old life as a doctor, finding much to enthrall him.

She strolled back to the vicarage, in no particular rush. Mrs. Chatterbucks and Miss Graves were walking back from the direction of the vicarage. 'You have a visitor,' said Mrs. Chatterbucks, smiling secretively.

'Oh dear, we were not supposed to say,' said Miss Graves. 'But it is a fine carriage, is it not?'

Elizabeth presumed they meant her aunt had called. Lady Bedlington had been far more sociable of late, having decided she was not ill after all. As such, she threw herself into the community with gusto. Whether the community wanted her constant interference into affairs it had managed quite well without her for many years, was another matter, but as the matriarch of the area, no one dared tell her that.

She saw the carriage when she was about a hundred yards from the vicarage. It was a fine carriage, but not her aunt's. She saw a figure come out of the vicarage door and look down the street towards her. He wore light trousers and a cream-coloured jacket, more suited to tropical climes.

'Elizabeth . . . ' She saw his lips form her name, and her heart did a triple somersault. The basket fell to the floor, breaking the eggs and scattering the flour, but Elizabeth did not care. She ran to Liam's outstretched arms.

'I thought you had forgotten me,' she said, when he had finished kissing her.

'No, my love. I was going to tell you I was coming, but I just needed to get here. I wanted to be sure I was free of the ghost of Christmas past before sullying our love with her presence. And now I am, and we can many. You will marry me, won't you?'

'Oh yes!' Oblivious to people watching from the street, including the sisters, who had turned back to watch the romantic drama unfold, she kissed him.

'I want you to know I'll be true to

you. I am not the man I led you to believe at your aunt's Christmas ball. A man who would deceive the wife he vowed to love. I would not for one minute offer you anything other than my utter devotion.'

'And I want you to know,' said Elizabeth lowering her voice so that the spectators couldn't hear, but answering the longing in her whole body, 'that I intend to be your wife in every way. I mean . . . ' She blushed, afraid he would think her too forward. Instead, she saw the same hunger in his eyes that she knew shone in hers.

'Then the sooner your father marries us the better,' he said in a husky voice, before kissing her again. 'Do you think he'll do it today?'

'I'm sure he would if we asked.'

'Or do you want to wait? Have a proper wedding, and the wonderful dress you deserve? Not that you don't look utterly beautiful in the one you're wearing.'

'I want to be your wife now, today,'

she said. 'I've waited long enough.'

'I love you, Elizabeth Dearheart,' he cried out, picking her up in his arms and spinning her around. 'My dear heart . . . And now I can let the whole world know it!'

The sisters watched from afar, each with a smile on her face.

'Well I never,' said Miss Graves dreamily.

'No, dear, I don't suppose you ever did,' said Mrs. Chatterbucks.

THE END

NIGHT MUSIC

Margaret Mounsdon

Marian, a talented concert pianist, and Georges, a tempestuous conductor known as the 'bad boy' of classical music, are deeply in love . . . That is, until their relationship — and even their very lives — are threatened when Marian's secret past, and her troubled sister, both catch up with her. Will she and Georges survive?